A CRITERION BOOK

FOR YOUNG PEOPLE

 # THE MAGIC DRUM

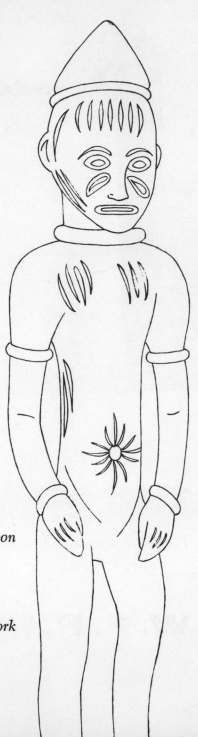

Illustrated by Ralph Thompson

Criterion Books   New York

THE MAGIC DRUM

Tales from Central Africa

W. F. P. Burton

CONTENTS

PREFACE

The following fables will doubtless come as a surprise to some who think that everyone who has not been educated by European standards is an "uncivilized" barbarian. For our standard of education is supposed to indicate the degree of a nation's civilization.

For centuries the Congo native has had a most accurate and efficient teaching system. It fits a native for adult life and is the product of the needs of the Central African environment and the demands of Central African youth. It shows him the part he should play in his relations with other people and his responsibility to the community. It gives him an accurate knowledge of the trees, animals and insects of the forests in which he lives. He receives the rudiments of geography, tribal history, medicine and many other branches of knowledge and handicrafts.

Of course much of the work of the blacksmith, gardener, builder, fisherman, hunter and canoe carver is learned by imitation. The son makes his tiny bow and arrows and follows his father to the forest or to the lakeside. The little girl takes her hoe and accompanies her mother to the fields, or, during the heat of the day, lends a hand in rendering palm oil, weaving baskets and preparing food.

But quite apart from "education by imitation" there is a beautiful system of instruction which is applied in the quiet of the evening about the fireside.

Luban village life is most efficiently organized. Each chief has his counselors or *bamfumu*, often up to twenty-five in number, and each counselor has his title and duties. Order of precedence and respect for superiors are most punctiliously observed, and the whole of court etiquette has evolved from age-long custom.

The *bamfumu* once held the power of death, and even today they are regarded as far above the ordinary villagers. They are to a large extent entrusted with advising the chief, regulating village life, and instructing the young.

Before they will display their stores of lore and learning, the dignity and reserve of some of these old aristocrats must be melted by gifts from the younger generation. Others, however, delight in interesting the children, and talk around the fireside is as much a source of satisfaction to them as to their listeners. They deliberately select the most attractive forms of teaching, wrapping up an otherwise objectionable pill in so much sugar-coating that their hearers are unaware of how much sound teaching they are assimilating.

The *bamfumu* often specialize in one particular branch of learning. Thus the *balute*, or "men of memory" as the village historians love to be called, can go back over two or three centuries of Luban history and tell of successions and wars, early customs and tribal boundaries, migrations and changes.

Careful questioning of native historians in villages as much as a month's journey apart shows how remarkably the histories agree, and how accurate are the memories of these old men, although, as their records are entirely oral, it is only to be expected that they should differ on minor details.

Others pride themselves on their proverbs and sayings, and are so apt with them that they are the staple of almost all their conversation. To the uninitiated, it sounds like a strange and unintelligible form of "stump oratory." There are thousands of proverbs, each consisting of two parts. In law cases and similar proceedings the orator throws out the first part of his proverb as a sort of challenge, and his listeners shout back the second in reply.

Much geography and natural history is learned by memorizing short couplets. Every tree and animal, every hill and stream, has an appropriate couplet describing its main features.

Thus, just as an American child naturally thinks of a sheep, cat or frog in connection with the nursery rhymes "Baa-baa black sheep," "Pussycat, pussycat, where have you been?" and "A frog he would a-wooing go," so a Luban child can unhesitatingly repeat hundreds of couplets describing, for instance, the villages beyond the Luvidyo River, the uses of the mulolo tree, the weather to be expected in February, the dangers of the kongolo snake, or the best bait for catching sendji rats.

These couplets have been heard over and over again until they have become part of the child's nature. A Luban boy of twelve can readily distinguish between two hundred different trees and describe the various uses of their leaves, bark, fruit, wood or roots, just as he can name as many different birds at sight or from their notes. He can also describe many of the habits of the more common animals, and the kind of trap with which they may be caught. He can give native remedies for a dozen different maladies, and knows the right month for sowing and harvesting the various crops. In fact these fireside chats give him a thorough and efficient start in his forest life.

In addition to the kind of teaching I have just described, there are various modes of social intercourse which most white people learn either from religious precept or from the hard knocks of life. The old *bamfumu* know that to teach such things in dry, formal platitudes, would be neither agreeable nor effective, so they give them the more palatable form of the fable.

Even in America, to make a point we do not need to recite the whole fable. When we call someone a "dog in the manger," or declare that a financier has "killed the goose that laid the golden eggs," the fables are so well known that the titles alone are enough to indicate the meaning. Similarly, in Lubaland the bare mention of "the dove's eggs in the gale," or of "the nightjar's big mouth," will often carry a point home far more forcibly than an hour's reasoning.

The African is the prince of fabulists, and students of native language and lore have done excellent service in collecting his tales. But in reading some of these collections one gets the impression that they are like a bouquet of beautiful flowers without the foliage, or a handful of loose gems without a setting. The real purpose of instruction, which originally called forth the fables, has been neglected. In retelling some of them in colloquial English I have therefore tried as far as possible to preserve the object their narrators had in mind when they originally told them across the logs of the open fire.

14

I have been tempted to delete much of the repetition with which the stories abound, but to do so entirely would be to rob them of one of their strongest attractions, at least in native minds. The little, wide-eyed, shivering youngsters around the village fires wait as eagerly for the inevitably repeated call of the lion to dinner, or the lame excuse of the tortoise, as we ourselves did for the "Fee-fi-fo-fum, I smell the blood of an Englishman," which made so deep an impression in the giant stories of our own childhood.

These fables are not the isolated product of a few local celebrities. They are as well known in Lubaland as "The Three Bears" or "Cinderella" in the nurseries of America, and may be heard any evening around the fires of any Luban village.

My only regret is that in our stereotyped, cut-and-dried English I cannot express all the beauties that are brought out by a native storyteller. To be heard at their best, the fables must be told by the old, half-naked, Luban *bamfumu* through the smoke of a village fire, with the dark forest trees as a background, and to the accompaniment of chirping crickets, the croaking of frogs in the stream, and the distant call of the jackal and hyena.

 # THE MAGIC DRUM

 **THE MAGIC DRUM**

The three younger boys prided themselves on their quick wits and were always taking a mean advantage of the oldest, who was slow, good-natured, and immensely strong. They would say, "Umpume, whatever would you do without us?" To which he would reply with a smile, "Perhaps some day you may even be glad of my help. At least you're glad to dance to my drumming." For he was a marvelous drummer.

They all went into the forest to hunt, putting up a temporary lodge of poles and grass in which to sleep and store the meat as they dried it on racks over slow fires.

19

They would select the lightest loads, such as the legs of the animals killed, and would leave him to bring in the rest of the carcass. Then they would cut the daintiest portions to cook for themselves, leaving him to gnaw the scraps off the bones. He only smiled.

One night as they slept there was a commotion outside the hunting lodge, and they looked out to find the head chief with his warriors.

"Who is there?" he called.

"We are huntsmen," replied the younger men, leaving Umpume apparently asleep.

"Whose is all this meat?"

"It belongs to our children."

"Give it all to me."

"We cannnot give away what is not ours."

"Then I will eat all your children," threatened the chief.

"Rather take the meat," they said, and the chief's warriors carried away every scrap.

In the morning they accused Umpume and thrashed him, but he said, "If I read the tracks in the dust aright, the chief was here in the night, and he nearly ate you." He had silently listened to all that had taken place.

After next day's hunting they decided to mount guard at night over the meat that was drying on the racks. Once more the chief came, and finding the three younger men sitting around the fire he went to see who was in the hut, whereupon Umpume, reaching out from the darkness, seized a glowing brand and pushed it into the chief's face. The chief fled, declaring furiously, "I'll fetch my warriors, cut you all up and dry your meat over those racks. You've burned the whiskers off my face."

"Umpume, what shall we do?" they asked in terror. "You have insulted his majesty with your firebrand and we are all doomed to die."

"Don't worry," said Umpume, smiling, "I will save you."

20

And while they hid the dried meat in a hollow tree, he carved a great drum. Then he put them into it, stretched a skin over the top, and taking a pointed digging stick and gourd in one hand and the drum under the other arm, as soon as light dawned he set out for home.

After a time he came face to face with a lion. "Where are you going?" said the lion.

"I come from home and I'm going home."

"Why do you carry these things?"

"The digging stick is for rooting out wild sweet potatoes and the gourd is for drinking water."

"And why carry a drum?"

"So that if anyone is sad-hearted I can drum for his dancing and send him away happy." With this Umpume sat down and rapped the drum so skillfully that the lion danced all around him in a circle and went away saying, "That is a nice fellow. He has put me in a good temper."

Then Umpume met a leopard. "Where are you going?" asked the leopard.

"I come from home and I'm going home."

"Why carry the digging stick and gourd?"

"The stick is for rooting out sweet potatoes and the gourd for drinking water."

"And why carry the drum?"

"So that if anyone is agile he can dance to my drum." And Umpume sat down and rapped the drum so skillfully that the leopard danced all around him in a circle, and then went away saying, "That is a charming fellow. He has recognized my agility."

Soon Umpume came face to face with an elephant, who demanded, "Where are you going?"

"I come from home and I'm going home."

"Why carry the digging stick and gourd?"

"The stick is for unearthing wild sweet potatoes and the gourd for drinking water."

"What purpose does the drum serve?"

"So that if anyone is stiff in the knees he may dance to my drumming and loosen his joints."

With this he put down his drum and played it so well that the elephant danced all around him in a circle and went away saying, "That is a splendid fellow. He has cured my stiff knees."

The same thing occurred with the buffalo, the wart hog and the crocodile.

Finally Umpume came face to face with the head chief and his warriors, all in a terrible rage. The chief did not recognize him as the man who had poked the glowing firebrand in his face, for that had occurred at night and in the darkness of the hunting lodge.

"Where are you going?" asked the chief.

"I come from home and I'm going home."

"Then why carry the digging stick and the gourd?"

"To provide myself with sweet potatoes for dinner and water to drink."

"What purpose does the drum serve?"

Umpume did not say that he had three trembling brothers inside the drum, but setting it down he said, "I drum for those who are in a rage, that they may give vent to their feelings and go home in peace."

With this he started to beat out a war dance, while the chief and his warriors leaped all around him in a frenzied circle of revenge, declaring that they would gnaw the very bones of those who had singed the chief's beard.

Gradually Umpume changed his measure until they danced around him in an ecstasy of rhythm, and finally his drum took on a tone of peace and satisfaction so that when he ceased to drum, the warriors ceased to dance, and the chief was so charmed that he quite forgot that he was on an expedition of revenge. He rewarded Umpume with a gun and sent him on his way remarking, "That is a delightful fellow. He has soothed my feelings."

When he arrived home, Umpume undid the drum skin and let his brothers out. They saluted him by rubbing earth on their chests in abject respect and said, "Umpume, you have saved us from the lion, the leopard, the elephant and all the other animals, and finally from the wrath of the head chief and his warriors. We are ashamed for having treated you so meanly, and henceforth we will give you your rightful place as head of the family."

Umpume did not say, "I told you so!" for that would not have been polite. He just kept on smiling.

THE LAZY MAN
AND THE WATER SPIRIT

Mulele was an African who lived in the Congo forest with his old mother. He was so idle that he could scarcely be persuaded to hunt even enough food to keep them alive, but always urged his mother to make more and more beer. When she chided him he said, "Oh, why was I not born a chief, with plenty of servants to wait on me, and everything I need brought to me without having to work for it?"

His mother replied, "My lazy son, you have not enough self control to be a chief, for if a man cannot control himself, how can he be expected to control his subjects? Rather go and set your traps, that we may have something to eat."

Mulele went off into the forest, and that evening he caught a guinea fowl.

As he passed the river on his way home, the water spirit

called, "Mulele, throw me in your food, and if you obey me you shall have food, and all else that you require."

Mulele threw the guinea fowl into the water with a splash. When he reached home his mother scolded him for not bringing back enough food, but Mulele took no notice, for he could think of nothing but the promise of the water spirit that he should have all that he required.

Next day he again went into the forest, and he caught a partridge. As he passed the river bank, the water spirit called once more, "Mulele, throw me in your partridge and you shall have all that you require."

Mulele threw in the bird with a splash. The water began to ripple and foam, while a voice called from the depths, "Mulele, all I ask of you is that you should show enough self control to tap the dance drums with your hands like a chief, and not with drumsticks like a poor man. Then all shall be yours."

Mulele promised, thinking that he had made a very easy bargain. Now the water became redder and redder, until Mulele saw a great gaping mouth which called, "Reach down into me, Mulele, and pull out all you find."

He reached down and pulled out a gourd; he reached down again and pulled out a second; he reached down again and pulled out a third, and a fourth, until the river bank was heaped with the big, sealed gourds. The spirit of the waters told him to break them on the great, flat rock at the back of his mother's hut, when he would receive all that he desired.

When he reached home, his mother taunted him for bringing home such useless rubbish, but when he broke the first gourd, out came a row of strong, handsome youths, who greeted him as their chief. When he broke the second, out came a row of beautiful maidens, who greeted him as their husband and master. When he broke the third, out came a pile of splendid clothing, which he and his mother ex-

changed for the wretched monkey skins that they were wearing. He broke the fourth gourd, and out came a pile of warm blankets. He broke the fifth, and out came stacks of hunters' guns. He broke the sixth, and out came kegs and kegs of gunpowder. He broke the seventh, and out came rows and rows of beautiful beads, blue and white. But if you heard of all that he broke, and of all that came out, it would take days to tell. Mulele received all that he desired. He was at last a great chief, with wives, soldiers, gardens, flocks, clothes, musical instruments. In fact, he lacked nothing.

He and his mother lived in the greatest pomp, waited on by hundreds of loyal and willing hands, but his taste for beer still remained. For much of the time he was so tipsy that he could not attend to affairs of state, and before long his people began to despise him.

At last one day he called for a great dance, and, as was usual on such occasions, many huge jars of native beer were prepared. All went well until Mulele became so excited and foolish, because his brain was made dizzy by the beer, that he snatched the drumsticks from a drummer and beat a loud "Ngudi-ngungu, ngidi-ngididi."

Before he could drum any more a bang was heard, the loudest bang that Mulele had ever heard. His head swam, his eyes watered, and his mind reeled. When everything about him became clear again, his beautiful robes of state and his mother's flowing dress had disappeared, and instead the old monkey skins suddenly appeared. The dancers had changed to waving grass, the blankets to fallen leaves, and once more he found himself thin, half-starved and dirty.

"Didn't I tell you," shrieked his mother, "that you have not enough self control to be a chief!"

Poor Mulele! It took him many days to get over his terrible loss, but at last he thought of going again to the water spirit. Setting out for the forest, he caught a gray wildcat and a brown wildcat, and took them to the river bank, where he shouted, "Spirit of the waters, shall I throw them in?"

"You may if you like, and you need not if you do not want to," answered the' water spirit very indifferently.

Mulele threw them in.

Next day he went once again to the forest, and he caught a gray wildcat and a brown wildcat. He took them to the river, and shouted, "Water spirit, may I throw them in?"

"You may if you wish, and you need not if you do not want to," said the water spirit.

"May I get some more of those gourds from your mouth?"

"You may if you wish, and you need not if you do not want to."

Mulele eagerly threw in the animals that he had caught. The waters began to ripple and foam. Then, as Mulele looked, he saw the great red mouth and, plunging in his arm, eagerly pulled out first one gourd and then another, until he had a great pile of them on the bank.

Breathlessly he carried them home. Then he broke the first on the rock that was behind his mother's hut. To his horror, out came a black snake, which darted at him.

Mulele thought that the next gourd might be more successful, but when he broke it, out came a crocodile, which snapped at him.

He was brokenhearted, but determined to try a third. When he broke it, however, out came a scorpion, which lifted up its poisoned tail at him. And when he broke a fourth, a centipede crawled out and ran toward him.

His mother was furious, and shouted, "Mulele, I want no such gifts near my hut. Off you go, and throw all the gourds back into the river."

Mulele sadly returned to the bank and threw back the remaining gourds. The spirit of the waters opened his great red mouth, swallowed down the gourds, and then called, "Mulele, you have seen how useless it is to give ease and wealth to those who have not worked for it. Let me advise you to work hard and practice self control, then you will enjoy a peace which can never be gained as a reward for idleness and folly."

Mulele took this advice and returned with a will to his traps and his garden. Although he never again became a chief, he and his mother had all that they needed of food and clothing, which, after all, is better than living in foolish luxury.

THE MAN WHO ALWAYS HELPED THE NEEDY

Kaleme the kind one was the twentieth son of his father, who was headman of the village. All his brothers married nice wives and thought of nobody's comfort or pleasure but their own. The hungry remained hungry, the lame received no helping hand, and the blind were never led, except by Kaleme.

His father and brothers always despised and grumbled at him, but still Kaleme could not bear to pass a person or animal in distress.

At last all the girls in the village were married except a leper, so Kaleme took the leper woman as his wife.

"Why do you take a wretched leper woman home?" cried his father and brothers together.

"It's no business of yours. I'm taking her to my home, not yours," answered Kaleme.

On another day, when a dog had stolen a piece of meat

29

and was about to be killed, Kaleme redeemed it for a piece of cloth and took it home.

"Why do you take home a thieving cur?" cried his father and brothers.

"I'm not taking it to your houses, but to mine."

Soon after, a hawk, having stolen a chicken, was caught in a trap, and the villagers were about to kill it when Kaleme took pity on it and redeemed it for another fowl.

"Fancy redeeming a useless hawk for a fine plump fowl," cried his father and brothers. "What will the silly fellow do next?"

"It's not your business, but mine," he answered.

Next day a rat that had nibbled at somebody's cloth was being tortured to death, when Kaleme saw what was going on, and his compassion was so aroused that he offered five francs to set the rat at liberty, and it followed him home.

His father and brothers were more angry than ever, and grumbled, "Now we can see that you are a fool, for you have thrown away five francs on a useless and rascally rat."

"That's my business," he said. "You prefer to spend your money on yourselves, but I like to see mine making others happy."

Walking through the village one day, Kaleme heard a shout and saw people running to kill a snake. His sympathy was aroused once more, and, offering his necklace of beads in exchange for the life of the snake, he took it home.

"Well, this beats everything," sneered his father and brothers. "Kaleme has taken home a leper, a thieving dog, a hawk, a useless rat, and now he has added a snake to his household. The soft-hearted fool! What will become of him?"

When Kaleme reached home he was surprised to see the snake stand up on its tail, and two neat feet appear. He was still more surprised to hear a man's voice saying, "Kaleme, I am the son of a great king. A cruel wizard bewitched me and turned me into a snake until such time as someone

30

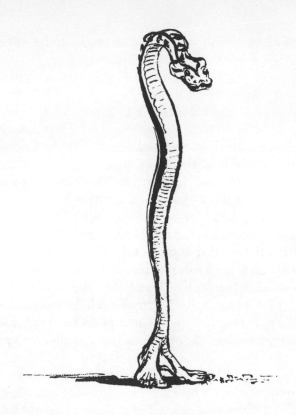

should have mercy upon me. Kaleme, I thought that nobody ever had mercy on a snake, and that I was condemned to crawl about in the dust forever and ever, but today by your kindness you have broken the charm of the wizard and I have become a man once more. Tomorrow I want you to come to my father's kingdom and he will reward you with whatever you want."

Next day they set out, and now the snake had become a young man, beautifully dressed in a colored loincloth, with omanda shells and beads around his neck—in fact with every sign of royal blood.

On the road young Prince Nyoka (for that was his name) told Kaleme, "If my father offers you a kingdom, refuse it.

If he offers you a thousand wives, refuse them. If he offers you the most beautiful wife in the world, refuse her. If he offers you his royal rings, refuse the first, refuse the second, refuse the third, refuse the fourth, refuse the fifth, refuse the sixth, but accept the seventh. It is a little ugly, bent, iron ring."

After a long journey they reached the largest town that Kaleme had ever seen. Crowds of people thronged the streets to welcome back their lost prince. The king, when he heard of Kaleme's kindness, gave him a splendid hut, and ordered a sumptuous banquet to be prepared.

Days of feasting and dancing followed, but at last Kaleme grew tired even of this and longed to go back home. The king called him aside and offered him a kingdom. Kaleme said that he would not accept it. He offered him a thousand wives, or the most beautiful wife in the whole world, but Kaleme said, "No, I have my own wife and do not want any more, for where there are many wives there is much quarreling."

Then the king offered him a lovely twisted wire brass ring, and Kaleme refused that. The king then brought out a succession of rings of silver and ivory, but Kaleme refused them all, until at last he produced an ugly little iron ring, all rusted with age and twisted so as to seem useless. It was the seventh ring. Kaleme bowed and accepted it with thanks.

The king seemed very surprised, but said, "Kaleme, you have done well in your choice, for you have only to lay this ring on the sick and they will become well; and if you rub it and wish, you will at once receive your every desire. But be warned of one thing. Never allow a strange woman in your house, or you may lose all."

When Kaleme returned to his home the first thing he did was to put the ring on his wife, and all the leprosy vanished, leaving her the most beautiful woman in the village. He now wished for friends to come and rejoice with him, and, unconsciously rubbing the ring, to his wonder he found himself surrounded by merry crowds of people. He wished that instead of living in dirty hovels, his fellow villagers should make pleasant huts, and they set to work on the spot to make a most beautiful village, with fruitful gardens. Everyone joined in making Kaleme king— No! Not everyone. For his father and brothers, when they saw how his kindness had been rewarded, were more jealous and cruel than ever, and seemed to hate especially his rat, his hawk, and his dog.

One day Kaleme heard crying down by the river, and it touched his kind heart. Going out, he found a poor half-starved woman who had just landed from a canoe and was being beaten by his brothers. In the kindness of his heart he quite forgot about the warning of the king who had given him the ring, and invited the woman into his home for shelter and food.

The woman showed great gratitude for all the kindness that Kaleme and his wife lavished on her. She was amazed at his beautiful house and village. At last her eyes lit on the ring, and going up to him she said, "What a funny little old ring! May I look at it?"

"Certainly," said Kaleme as he offered it to her. Just at that moment a boat drum beat, and the woman, starting at the sound, rushed out of the house with Kaleme's ring to where a big canoe filled with men and women and with rows of paddlers had silently drawn up to the bank. She jumped in, and away went the canoe with the woman and the ring, leaving poor Kaleme behind.

When he returned home he found that all his friends had run away, his village was in ruins, and his wife's leprosy was worse than ever before. All that was good and happy in his life had vanished, while his father and brothers only laughed at him and told him that it was what he deserved for being so softhearted.

As he sat on the bank in despair, the hawk and the rat asked him what was wrong. He pointed to the fast-disappearing canoe, telling them how his ring of good fortune had been stolen.

At once the hawk lifted the rat in his talons and, flying off with him, dropped him onto the end of the great canoe, saying, "Rat, when you have found the ring, climb back to the end of the canoe. I will swoop and pick you up."

The rat wriggled into all the corners, examined all the cloth, searched all the baskets, looked over all the people, and at the same time kept himself so carefully out of sight that nobody knew that there was a rat in the boat. Then when he found the little iron ring he leaped onto the end of the boat, and before anyone could move, the hawk swooped down and carried him away in his talons.

As they were flying toward Kaleme's village, the hawk said, "I will give Kaleme the ring. It will be a suitable reward for his having rescued me from death."

"No indeed!" cried the rat. "I found the ring, and Kaleme rescued me too. It is I who should return it to him."

"Well now, I will show you that you cannot get home at all without my help," said the hawk in anger. And flying far away into the forest, he dropped the rat and the ring, and then returned to tell Kaleme that both rat and ring were lost.

Poor Kaleme's heart was sorer than ever, for he loved his wife and wished to heal her of her leprosy. As he sat sadly with his head in his hands, his little dog came to him and said, "Master, I have a nose that can smell things however far away they are. I will find your ring."

He went and he sniffed. He sniffed and sniffed. For days he did nothing but follow the scent of the ring, until far away in the forest he found the little rat, nearly dead from starvation, but with the ring still in his mouth.

Then taking both rat and ring in his teeth, the little dog ran so fast that before night fell he had placed both at his master's feet.

Without delay Kaleme took the ring and healed his wife. Then he rubbed it, and his friends returned in such numbers that he was more popular than before. Even his father and brothers softened their hearts toward him.

After this Kaleme and his wife always lived happily, and they had many little sons and daughters to brighten their home. But they would never again allow a strange woman to enter their hut, and to the end of his days Kaleme continued his kindness to both men and animals.

THE MAN WHO WAS ALWAYS BORROWING AND LENDING

Wakwajima never had any tools of his own, and he was always poor, because whatever he needed he would borrow from others.

His poor distracted wife often pleaded with him, "Husband, why don't you keep your own tools and let other folk keep theirs? Take my advice or we shall always be dependent upon others."

Wakwajima began to clear away the forest for a garden down by the river, and asked the chief for the loan of a bush knife with which to cut down the tangled creepers that hung from tree to tree. But alas! His hand slipped, and the knife fell into the river and disappeared.

Wakwajima spent the rest of the day diving, paddling and feeling with feet or hands, but toward sunset he had to go and confess to the chief, "I'm sorry, but your knife has fallen in the river and I cannot find it."

"Lying thief," roared the chief. "You have stolen my bush knife and hidden it. If you do not return it within three days, I will sell your wife and children as slaves."

When Wakwajima went home and told his wife the bad news, she was deeply grieved and said, "Husband, I have always given you good advice. If you had only stopped borrowing and lending, we should not be in this terrible trouble."

Next morning he was down at the river early, groping about among the reeds and water weeds, contemplating suicide, when a strange thing happened.

A messenger fish, dressed in its indigo trousers and red fez, rose to the surface, saluted with its fin, and called, "My master the King of the Fishes has sent me to tell you, Wakwajima, that your knife is found, and if you come to his underwater city, he will return it to you. Come!"

The fish started off downstream. Wakwajima dived in and followed. He was amazed to find that by stretching his fingers before him and his toes behind him, he could go faster and faster and faster, past reeds and rocks, under waterfalls and through oyster beds, till they came to a marvelous city under the water, with a great palace surrounded by houses and guarded by soldier fish with bayonets on their guns. And Wakwajima saw many strange fish of varieties he had never seen before.

The messenger fish went inside the palace and bowed before a throne, on which sat a great mudfish. Wakwajima bowed too, and was shocked when it barked at him, "Get up, you fool!"

Then, as it fixed its great goggle eyes on him, it said, "Wakwajima, you are a silly man. Why don't you heed your wife's counsel and stop your borrowing and lending. Your knife has been found and brought to me. Here it is. Now go home and get your own tools, and leave other people to enjoy theirs. He who would borrow will only swamp himself with lawsuits and trouble."

Wakwajima took his leave and thanked the King of the Fishes, but as he was going the king said, "Wakwajima, not many people from the upper world come to my underwater kingdom, so as a souvenir of your visit I am giving you a hunting dog," and he gave him the most extraordinary looking animal Wakwajima had ever seen.

Wakwajima thanked him and was leading the dog away by a string when the King of the Fishes called after him, "Treat it well. Only send it after one animal a day. It will catch anything you send it after, but if you send it after more than one animal a day it will return to me."

"Come," ordered the messenger fish, and started back upstream.

Wakwajima and the dog followed faster and faster, faster, fas fas fas fafafa, past crocodiles and water snakes, hippopotami and fish, until he scrambled out just where he had dived in.

He first returned the bush knife to the chief. Then, going into the forest with his dog, he set it on a wild pig. One leap and the pig was down and kicking its last.

Wakwajima made his wife and children a feast, and with the remainder he bought an axe, a hoe, a bush knife and baskets, determined to have tools of his own.

Next day he was out again in the forest and returned with an antelope. Indeed, every day saw fresh meat brought in, so that Wakwajima and his dog became famous.

Then one day the chief called him, and said, "Wakwajima, lend me your hunting dog."

"Oh, but I mustn't borrow or lend."

"Nonsense! I lent you my bush knife. Now you must lend me your dog."

What could the poor man say? He only pleaded, "I will lend you my dog if you will promise only to send it after one animal a day."

"I promise," said the chief, and immediately forgot.

They went into the forest and there stood a buffalo.

"Catch it!"

The dog gave one leap, caught the buffalo by the throat and hung on.

The buffalo bellowed and screamed with rage but could not shake off the dog, and the hunters rushed in and finished it with their spears.

On their way home they came face to face with a great elephant, and before Wakwajima could stop him, the chief shouted, "Catch him!"

The dog leaped at the elephant, bringing it to its knees, and the hunters killed it.

Then to Wakwajima's dismay the dog gave a wild yelp and dashed toward the river.

"Hi, hi, hi! Come back! Come back!" But all Wakwajima's calling and whistling did not stop it. It plunged into the river and disappeared.

Wild with grief, Wakwajima stood on the bank wondering what to do, when a strange thing happened. A messenger fish, dressed in its indigo tunic, a red fez on its head, rose to the surface, saluted Wakwajima with its fin, and called, "My master, the King of the Fishes, has sent me to thank you for the return of the hunting dog, and he leaves you just one warning. Take your wife's advice and stop borrowing and lending."

Then it disappeared into the depths of the river.

THE HONEY GATHERER'S THREE SONS

A honey gatherer had three sons, all born at the same time. Their names were Hear-it-however-faint-the-sound, Follow-it-however-great-the-distance and Put-it-together-however-small-the-pieces. These names are sufficient to indicate the skill of these young men, but their friends called them simply Hear, Follow and Piece.

One day the honey gatherer went on a long, long journey into the forest until he came to a tree that was as high as a hill, and the bees that buzzed in and out showed clearly that it must be full of honey. He climbed up, but, treading on a rotten branch, fell to the ground and was broken into ten pieces.

Hear was sitting beside the hut in the village, but he promptly jumped to his feet, saying, "Father has fallen from a tree. Come! Let us go to his help."

His brother Follow set out and led them along the father's tracks until they came upon the body lying in ten pieces. Piece then put all the parts together, fastened them up, and the father walked home while the sons carried his honey.

Next day the honey gatherer again set out to look for honey, while his sons sat at home, each boasting that he was more important than the others.

"You could not have heard him without me," said Hear.

"Though you had heard him you could not have found him without me," said Follow.

"Even though you had found him, you could not have put him together without me," said Piece.

Meanwhile, the old honey gatherer had gone far into the forest till he came to a tree as high as the clouds, and the bees buzzing in and out showed clearly that it must be full of honey. He climbed up, but, treading on a rotten branch, fell to the ground and was broken into a hundred pieces. His sons were sitting at home boasting about their prowess, when Hear jumped up, saying, "Father has fallen!"

Follow reluctantly set out to follow the footprints, and found the hundred pieces on the ground. Pointing to them he said, "See how indispensable I am. I have found him for you."

Piece then put the hundred pieces together very grudgingly, saying, "I, and I alone, have restored Father."

Their father walked home, while the sons carried the honey.

Next day the old honey gatherer went farther than ever into the forest and he found a tree that reached to the stars. The bees buzzing in and out showed that it must be full of honey. He climbed up, but, treading on a rotten branch, fell to the ground and was broken into a thousand pieces.

Hear heard the fall, but would not tell his brothers. Follow knew that there must have been an accident since his father did not return, while Piece realized that his father needed his assistance, but would not condescend to ask his brothers to find him so that he might piece him together.

So the old honey gatherer died, because the selfish sons each thought more of his own reputation than of his father's. In truth, each needed the others, and none was wiser or better than the rest.

THE LEOPARD AND THE BUSHBUCK BUY A DRUM

Nge the leopard was too poor to buy a drum, and one day he hit upon a cruel plan to get one.

He called upon Gulungu the bushbuck, and said, "If you will accompany me tomorrow we will go to the village market to exchange meat for a drum. Meet me at the crossroads at sunrise."

Promptly at sunrise Gulungu was at the crossroads, but

Nge, waiting till Gulungu had left his house, ran in with a basket and said, "Mrs. Gulungu, your husband wants to take the twins with him to the village. Put them in this basket."

The unsuspecting bushbuck's wife brought the children, still fast asleep, and helped to tie them safely in the basket, after covering them with grass. Then the leopard ran swiftly to the crossroads, and set out with Gulungu for the village.

Before they had gone very far, and while Gulungu was taking his turn at carrying the basket, the squirrel ran down from a tree and whispered in his ear, "Silly fellow! You are going to sell your own children for a drum."

When he heard this, the bushbuck decided he must open the basket. Beginning to limp, he said that there was a thorn in his foot and that he must stop to take it out. Then when the leopard was around the bend in the path, Gulungu untied the basket, peeped in, and there, sure enough, were his babies. He hurried back to his house, where he left the babies, and then called on Mrs. Nge. He told her that her husband, the leopard, wanted to take his cubs to the village, and packing them into the basket, Gulungu soon caught up with Nge along the path.

Near the village Nge thought to himself, "If Gulungu's twins awake and cry, my plan will be discovered."

So he said, "Gulungu, I think that the meat will sell better if it is cooked. Let us boil some water and pour it over the basket and its contents." Little did he know that he was killing his own cubs.

At the village market the basket of meat was soon exchanged for a drum, and Nge saw his friend, Gulungu, as far as the crossroads on his journey home. Then when Gulungu had gone some distance down the path Nge shouted, "Gulungu, you were a silly creature. You sold your own twins for a drum."

The bushbuck went off whimpering until he was a safe distance from the leopard, and then shouted, "Nge, I was not as silly as you, for you cooked your own cubs."

Nge rushed home and, sure enough, he found out his mistake. But it served him right, for he who would take a mean advantage of another will, sooner or later, be swindled himself.

THE LEOPARD AND THE BUSHBUCK GO HUNTING

For months Nge could think of nothing but taking revenge on Gulungu. Finally he pretended to make friends, and suggested that, to seal their renewed friendship, they should go on a hunting expedition together.

They decided on a camping site in the forest and Nge arranged to reach the place before Gulungu. Nge knew there was a water spring there, and as soon as he arrived he covered the spring with his bed mat.

The first day they killed an eland and brought it into camp. Nge said, "I will stay in camp to cut up the meat and prepare the porridge. You take this basket and bring water from the river."

Gulungu had always drunk water from the river, and did not know the difference between a basket and a pot, so, taking the basket to the river, he tried to carry it back full of water. But each time the water ran out of the holes in the basketwork.

Meanwhile, Nge filled his pot with water from beneath his bed mat, and cooked and ate his porridge. When Gulungu came back without water, Nge growled at him and pretended to be very hungry, but as they could not cook food without water, they lay down to sleep.

Next morning they went out again to hunt, and killed a wild pig. The bushbuck was again sent with the basket to fetch water, and in his absence Nge took more water from beneath his bed mat, made porridge, and ate it.

When Gulungu reached the river, Nkuvu the tortoise called out, "Gulungu, if you give me some of the white beans from your sides, I will give you some good advice."

Gulungu gladly parted with some of his spots, and to this day you may see the gaps on the bushbuck's sides, from which the beans were taken.

Then Nkuvu said, "Gulungu, if you want to carry water in a basket, you must first smear the inside with clay, but Nge is deceiving you, for he has hidden a spring of water beneath his bed mat. I will show you how to frighten him."

The tortoise reached up and took down the moon, hanging it around Gulungu's neck. He put the sun on his head, and covered his chest with stars.

(If you doubt that the tortoise is able to do this, go to the riverside on any sunny day, or starry night, and you will see where the tortoise's children play with the sun, the moon or the stars on the surface of the water.)

"Now," said Nkuvu, "rush at Nge the leopard, and he will think that you are Vidye Mubi, the Evil Spirit. Go and give him a fright."

Gulungu went screaming, shaking and gurgling down the path. When Nge saw him coming, he fell to the earth in horror, moaning, "Oh, Vidye Mubi, please don't kill me. Have mercy on me, and I will do whatever you want."

"MAKE ME PORRIDGE!" roared Gulungu.

"I have no water, and must wait till my friend Gulungu returns. Oh, please have patience, Vidye Mubi."

"It is not true, for there is water under your bed mat," roared Gulungu.

The water was boiled, and the meal poured in.

"I have nothing to stir it with," whined Nge.

"Stir it with your paws, and be quick about it or I will swallow you up."

Poor Nge put one paw into the boiling porridge and then hastily withdrew it.

"Stir it again!" shrieked Gulungu.

Reluctantly the other paw was put into the porridge, but quickly withdrawn.

Nge was forced to stir the porridge over and over again until both paws were so badly scalded that there was no skin left on them, and the flesh was swollen and painful.

Gulungu ate the porridge and went prancing wildly down the path.

When he reached the river bank, he hid the sun, the moon and the stars in the reeds, and, smearing the sides of his basket with clay, returned to find Nge prostrate with pain and fear.

"What is the matter?" Gulungu asked.

"What! Did you not see Vidye Mubi?"

"No, which way did he go?"

"Don't ask me, for my paws are so sore that I can think of nothing else. He ordered me to cook him porridge, and I had to stir it with my paws. Look!" and he held up his blistered paws.

"But where did you get your water?"

The leopard was much flustered before he could think of a reply. "I, er, um, I, well, yes. Oh, I found some in a hollow tree."

Gulungu and Nge went hunting next day and killed a porcupine. Nge remained to cut it up, while Gulungu went to fetch water, but as soon as he had reached the reeds by the river bank, he put on his sun, moon and stars, and came rushing up the path at Nge, who fell down terror-stricken.

The leopard groaned for mercy, and the bushbuck demanded porridge at once. When the water was boiled and the meal poured in, the leopard came cringing before Gulungu, pleading, "Please don't make me stir it, Vidye Mubi, for the skin is off my forepaws, and I have nothing else with which to stir the porridge."

"Stir it with your back paws."

The skin came off both back paws, and still the porridge was not ready. Gulungu flashed beams of fierce sunlight in the tear-filled eyes of Nge, and growled, "Grrrrrr! If you do not want me to kill you this moment, stir the porridge with your tail."

Now everyone knows how proud the leopard is of his beautiful spotted tail, but there was nothing Nge could do but obey, so in went the tail and off came the skin, and around stirred the porridge till the meal was cooked, after which Gulungu ate it and went buzzing off down the road like a swarm of hornets.

Soon after, Gulungu, stripped of the sun, moon and stars, came meekly into camp carrying a basketful of water.

"Have you seen Vidye Mubi?" Nge whined.

"No! What are you looking so glum about? And what is the matter with your tail?"

"Oh dear! I have barely escaped with my life. He has been here again, and made me stir the porridge with my tail."

"Where did you find the water?"

"I, er, well, that is, um, oh, some passers-by left it for me," answered Nge, taken aback by the question, and little knowing that his lies were known as soon as uttered. "Let us leave this place as soon as the sun rises tomorrow, for if Vidye Mubi finds me here again, he will kill me outright."

So, early in the morning the limping leopard set out for home, accompanied by Gulungu, who carried the basket of dried meat, and gloated over the success of his revenge.

When they bade each other goodbye at the crossroads Nge put his paw to his mouth and shouted, "Gulungu! Ha-ha! I made you carry water in a leaky basket."

Gulungu went some distance pretending to whimper, and then shouted, "Nge! Ha-ha-ha! I made you stir the porridge with your tail," and then, turning, he fled home with the basket of meat.

HE WHO IS FEARED BY ALL

The squirrel was looking for a new home in the forest, and, coming to a great tree, he took a fancy to the spot. He had never seen such great branches, or a place so quiet and cool, so he cut some poles for the beams of his new house and left them on the ground.

The leopard was also looking for a home, and that night, coming to the big tree, he thought to himself, "There never was so nice a place as this. It is just the spot for my new home. There are even poles on the ground with which I can make my walls and beams."

The leopard dug holes, and stuck the poles in for his walls.

Next morning the squirrel came to go on with his house, and was more delighted than ever, for somebody had built the walls in his absence. So he cut rafters and gathered bark rope for lacing them into position.

That evening the leopard came back and was surprised to find everything ready for his roof. He tied on the rafters with the bark rope that was made ready for him.

In the morning the squirrel returned and, to his joy, the roof was ready for thatching. "What a wonderful site for a house," he thought. "Why, the materials build themselves. I will now gather grass for the thatch, and tomorrow I can bring my wife and children here."

In the evening the leopard arrived, and was so pleased to find the bundles of grass ready that he quickly thatched his roof.

Next morning the squirrel brought his children, and was delighted to find the house all nicely thatched and ready for him.

As he left his children to go back for the cooking pots and for the skins on which to sit, the squirrel said, "My children, if anyone comes in my absence and asks whose house this is, or who your father is, tell him I am HE WHO IS FEARED BY ALL."

The squirrel had not been gone long when the leopard came to finish his house, and, on finding the children spinning tops, he said, "Whose children are you?"

"We are the children of HE WHO IS FEARED BY ALL."

48

"Well, well! I must be careful," thought the leopard. "Who is there that is feared by all? They fear the lion, the elephant, the crocodile and the hippopotamus. They fear the buffalo and the rhinoceros, but who is this that all men fear?"

The leopard went to the elephant, and said, "O King, who is this that has settled in your domain, and is named HE WHO IS FEARED BY ALL?"

"Go and fetch him to me that he may pay me tribute and do me homage," said the elephant.

Meanwhile, the squirrel had carried in the skins and had gone off for the cooking pots.

The leopard returned to the big tree and asked for HE WHO IS FEARED BY ALL.

"Father is out leopard hunting," answered the children. "Sit down and wait till he comes." They offered the leopard a leopard skin on which to sit, but he was so frightened of losing his life that he ran off to tell the news to the king elephant.

"*I* will make him pay tribute," roared the lion. "I fear no one. I seize with my teeth and tear with my claws. I will go to the big tree and bring him to you."

"Where is your father?" he asked the squirrel's children when he arrived.

"He's out lion hunting," they answered. "Sit down and wait till he comes."

They spread a lion skin for him to sit on, but the lion got such a terrible fright that he ran off to tell the news to the king elephant.

"*I* will make him pay tribute," bellowed the buffalo. "I break down trees with my weight, and toss my enemies high into the air on my horns. I fear nobody." And he went off to the big tree.

"Where is your father?" he asked the squirrel's children.

"He is out buffalo hunting. Sit down and wait till he returns." And they spread a buffalo skin for him to sit on,

but the buffalo got such a fright that he did not stop running till he reached the king elephant and told him what a terrible man was HE WHO IS FEARED BY ALL.

What was to be done? The elephant could not have so fearful a person in his domain. They must all go together, and either make him pay tribute or drive him out.

The elephant went, the lion went, the leopard went, the buffalo went, the hippo went, the python went. In fact, all the animals went and asked for HE WHO IS FEARED BY ALL.

"Father is in the garden. Sit down till he returns," said the squirrel's children. To the elephant they gave an elephant skin, to the lion they gave a lion skin, to the python they gave a python skin, to each animal a skin like his own.

As all sat waiting for the squirrel, they trembled to think of the prowess of him who had slain so many of their relatives and cured their skins.

When at last the squirrel came, with the greatest friendliness he invited them all to stay for a meal, but he whispered to his wife to put a luzokoma nut in each plate, and to cover it with mutton broth and meat.

Each animal enjoyed his mush, his broth and his meat, but when they came to the nut, the lion broke a tooth but could not break his nut, the buffalo hurt his mouth but could not break his nut, the leopard cut his lip, but could not break his nut. In fact, not one of the guests could break his nut.

"Well, this is strange," remarked the squirrel to his wife as he took his nut and cracked it. "They have eaten elephant meat. They have eaten lion meat. They have eaten buffalo meat. They have eaten leopard meat. And yet not one of them can break a luzokoma nut."

When all the animals saw the squirrel break the nut that had been too hard for them, and when they learned that they had eaten their relatives (though really they had only eaten mutton), they ran away from the squirrel's home in dismay, and declared that in future they would always be more polite to strangers, however small.

THE BAT WHO BELONGED
TO NO ONE

The fruit bat was dying beside the road, and those who passed and saw his plight called to the rats, saying, "A poor fellow is dying beside the road, and there is no one to go to his aid. Go quickly, for he must be a relative of yours. He has your teeth."

The rats ran to help him, but soon came away in disdain, saying, "He is no relative of ours, for although he has our teeth, we have no wings. Let the birds come and help him."

The birds came flying to help the stranger, but soon flew away in disgust, saying, "He is no relative of ours, for although he has our wings, his tail shows him to be of the antelope family. He has no feathers, but only fur."

The antelope ran to the dying stranger, but soon left him in scorn, saying, "He is no relative of ours. We can leap long distances, but not like this fellow. Why, we have seen him above the treetops. He must belong to the squirrels, for his hair is like theirs."

The squirrels were called to the side of the dying bat, but soon left him with contempt, saying, "Our family indeed! He is no such thing. Though he has our hair, we have not ugly arms like his."

Poor bat! He was neither one thing nor the other. No bird or animal would claim him, so he died all alone, and his bones rotted beside the road, despised by all and mourned by none.

Remember! Be one thing or the other.

THE BOY WHO CUT
EVERYTHING TO PIECES

Muchibi was so fond of cutting trees, fences, poles, and indeed everything that he could reach with his axe, that he got into trouble everywhere. He chopped down his father's palms and pawpaw trees, he destroyed his mother's hoe handle, and there seemed to be no way of curing him.

At last his father called a slave and told him to take Muchibi to Pieces Land and to leave him there.

It was a long journey, and before they reached the end Muchibi was very tired and thirsty. Then suddenly the slave ran off and left him all alone in the forest.

Muchibi tried to return by the path along which they had come, but after going a little way, it suddenly ended. He followed a side track, but that too was only a piece of a path. When he attempted to go forward again the path stopped suddenly.

Very tired and frightened, he looked for a tree to climb, but all the trunks seemed to end halfway up. They had twigs growing out of the leaves, instead of the other way around, and fruit or leaves growing on the trunk instead of bark, while the branches grew down into the ground and the roots were where the branches are generally found.

53

Presently he was horrified to see a row of heads and arms coming up from the river, all laughing and talking, but although they had their water pots on their heads, they had no bodies. He called them, and asked the way to the village, but although they began to answer him, they always stopped before they came to the end of a sentence.

At last it became more and more clear that Muchibi was in a land where everything was in pieces. He asked for water to drink, but they only gave him a piece of gourd and all the water ran out. He followed the heads to the village and was horrified to see arms and legs hoeing in the gardens.

It now became cloudy and the rain began to fall, so Muchibi ran to a hut for shelter, but he might as well have

54

remained outside, for the hut that he entered had only a wall, while those into which the heads and arms had gone were all thatch and no walls.

He intended to wait until dark and then to seek a more comfortable hut, but he soon found that morning would dawn in the afternoon, or that night would suddenly fall for a time during the day.

When a part of a young man took pity on him and gave him food, poor Muchibi could not satisfy his appetite, for he found that these people of Pieces Land did not eat mush and relish together, but divided up the meal, so that they often had a mush as it was growing light in the evening, or a relish as it was growing dark in the morning. These people did not carry axes or knives with which to cut their food or firewood, but a banana leaf full of gum with which to stick together the food and firewood, for it was already in such small pieces that it was impossible to carry.

Muchibi thought that he would die in this strange land. He wandered eastward toward the sunset or westward toward the sunrise, and he climbed when he wanted to go down, for pieces of the hills were down in the rivers and pieces of the streams ran up into the hills.

At last he flung himself down with his face in a tuft of grass in the tree tops and moaned, "If only I could return home I would never again cut up anything uselessly." At once his father's slave touched him on the shoulder and said, "Your father has sent for you to come home. Follow me."

Muchibi was so glad to get home that he ran all the way, but he was quite a different boy from the one who had left a few days before. He could not bear the sight of a knife or axe and was so pleased to find everything whole again that he could never be tempted to cut anything in pieces.

THE MOST USEFUL TREE
IN THE WORLD

The king overheard an argument about which was the most useful tree. People became angry about it. They struck each other and used abusive language. At last he said to himself, "Whichever tree is the most useful, it is clearly useless to raise such bitterness over a mere argument. I will give my people a lesson."

The king caused his drum to be beaten and all his subjects gathered together. Then he brought forth his youngest daughter, the most beautiful girl who had ever been seen. Chiefs' sons had married her elder sisters, and they had paid large gifts in guns, beads, omanda shells, blankets, cloth and gunpowder.

The king announced in a loud voice, "All my nine daughters are married. There only remains this tenth. I am sad at parting with her but the time has come for her to marry and to leave my home. I will not give her for wealth, nor will I give her for fame and position, but I have heard an argument in the village about which is the most useful tree. Now I myself will announce the name of the most useful tree to my son. I will describe its roots, its trunk, its branches and its leaves, and the one who can name that tree to me shall have my daughter Wadikumi."

Of course everyone thought that his favorite tree must

surely be the one, so that when the day for naming the tree arrived and people flocked from far and near at the sound of the drum, many hearts were sad as one after another named his tree and all were turned away. One favored the mutondo tree as it is useful for making canoes. Another chose the mujusu as it is soft for carving bowls. A third was sure that the mulolo must be the tree as it provides hoe and axe handles. But though hundreds of trees were mentioned, and each with some very practical use, the king said that none had chosen the best tree of all, and all alike were disappointed. They asked that another day might be given them, and that they all might try again.

Perhaps Nkumbi the muskrat was more sad than the rest, for he loved Wadikumi, tenth daughter of the king, and he longed to make her his own. Now Kamimbi the swallow and Nkumbi the muskrat were great friends, and, seeing his companion so glum, Kamimbi asked the reason.

Nkumbi answered, "Alas! I have failed to win Wadikumi, daughter of the king. I love her and long for her. Moreover, I felt sure that the manioc was the most useful tree, with porridge in its roots, soap ash in its trunk and vegetables for food in its leaves. It can be used as a dye or as a poultice, and will provide a refreshing drink, or, if treated differently, a violent poison. But the king says that there is an even more useful tree than manioc, and that if I cannot guess it I cannot have Wadikumi."

Kamimbi the swallow then hit on this plan. He said, "I will fly into the king's enclosure today, and will hear him tell his son the name of the tree. Then I will return and tell you, so that you may be sure that you have the right name."

As the crowds of baffled people returned sadly to their villages, Kamimbi glided silently into the chief's enclosure, and was just in time to hear him say to his son, "No one guessed the name of the tree today. The most useful tree is the mwabi, the tree of unselfishness. Its roots are Affection;

57

your friend loves you and you love him. Its trunk is Giving; your friend gives to you and you give to him. Its branches are Welcome; your friend welcomes you and you welcome him. And its leaves are Work; your friend serves you and you serve him. He who cultivates the mwabi will never abuse or get angry with his neighbor."

Noiselessly Kamimbi glided away from the king's enclosure, and flying to Nkumbi he whispered, "Nkumbi, I have the name of the tree. It is the mwabi, the tree of unselfishness. Its roots are Affection; your friend loves you and you love him. Its trunk is Giving; your friend gives to you and you give to him. Its branches are Welcome; your friend welcomes you and you welcome him. And its leaves are Work; your friend serves you and you serve him."

Nkumbi was so delighted that he could not sleep in his longing for the next day to dawn, that he might win his Wadikumi.

Early in the morning the royal drum sounded out the summons, and once more the eager crowds flocked to the king's enclosure, but although many learned men were there, nobody could think of the most useful tree until at last Nkumbi came forward in humble respect, dragging his long tail over the ground, and said, "My lord, the tree is the mwabi, the tree of unselfishness. Its roots are Affection; your friend loves you and you love him. Its trunk is Giving; your friend gives to you and you give to him. Its branches are Welcome; your friend welcomes you and you welcome him. And its leaves are Work; your friend serves you and you serve him."

The king rose and gave his beautiful daughter Wadikumi to Nkumbi, while the beating of the drums was deafening, and the crowds cheered and threw dust into the air, chalking Nkumbi all over with white chalk, and declaring that he had rightly guessed, and that there was nothing so valuable in the country as unselfishness.

Of course, there was no more quarreling about the most useful tree, but all began to cultivate the mwabi, tree of unselfishness. A great wedding feast was prepared for Nkumbi and his bride, at which Kamimbi, the friend of the bridegroom, was given the highest place at the banquet.

THE BUFFALO WHO MADE UNDUE DEMANDS

One day Mbo the buffalo set a pit trap in the forest, and Ntambo the lion fell into it. Next day, when the buffalo found the lion and was about to kill him, the lion pleaded, "Please have mercy on me and I will kill for you all the meat you need. Just release me, and all you have to do is say, 'Ntambo, I need a zebra' or 'Ntambo, I want an eland,' and I will see that you are well supplied."

Mbo released the lion, and Ntambo went straight off into the forest and killed him an eland, which Mbo and his friends much enjoyed.

The next time Mbo met Ntambo in the forest he announced, "This time I must have three big animals."

"I will be true to my promise even though I have my children to feed and what you ask is hard," said the lion, and he set off to hunt for Mbo's meat.

Presently Mbo heard him roaring, "Come! Come!" and, following the voice, he found that the lion had killed him a hartebeest, a sable and a roan antelope. Mbo took them home and enjoyed them with his friends.

Shortly afterwards, Mbo again met the lion and said, "Ntambo, get me ten big animals."

Ntambo answered, "Look how thin I am. I have scarcely had time to hunt for myself. Why are you not less demanding in what you ask?"

The buffalo, however, was so greedy that he insisted on ten, and held the lion to his promise.

Late that night he heard Ntambo calling, "Come! Come!" and, following the voice, he found ten great animals freshly killed for him, and Mbo enjoyed them with his friends.

Some time after this he came upon Ntambo crossing the plain, looking so thin that he was scarcely able to lope along. He said, "Please, Mbo, do not ask for more meat just yet. I will keep my promise, but I have killed so much for

you that I have had no time to hunt for myself and my children."

"I cannot help what you need," answered Mbo. "I must hold you to your word. Now go and get me one of every kind of animal in the forest."

"Very good," answered Ntambo. "Had you been sensible and thought of others besides yourself, you might always have had enough and to spare, but since you do not care whether I go hungry or not, I will carry out your orders. Your greed has been your downfall. You order me to seize one of each kind of animal in the forest, so I will start with you." And leaping upon the neck of the buffalo he dragged him to the ground and killed him.

THE MAN WHO TRIED
TO CATCH THE NIGHT

Two men once had a great argument concerning their skill in trapping and hunting. One boast led to another until they began to exaggerate, and at last one said that he could make such skillful basket traps that he could even catch the night.

When he was challenged to do so, he carefully plaited a basket trap of the most closely woven reeds, and in the evening set it in a dark corner of the forest, saying, "If I cannot catch the night with my hands, I will enclose it in my basket trap."

When the wind moaned in the treetops he shouted, "Who are you?"

The answer was, "I am the dusk," but although he ran until he knocked his shins against the trees in the gloaming, he caught nothing.

Sitting still beside his basket trap he heard the wind rustling in the reeds and shouted, "Who are you?"

"I am the twilight," rustled the wind, but although he ran until he scratched himself in the thorns, he caught nothing.

Returning to his trap once more he kept watch, and hearing the wind make the branches creak against each other he called, "Who are you?"

"I am time to go to bed," creaked the branches in the wind, but although he ran until he became tangled in the creepers, he caught nothing.

Wearily he groped his way back to the trap, and after waiting until his eyelids drooped he was suddenly awakened again by the wind raising ripples in the stream.

"Who are you?" he called desperately.

"I am midnight," replied the stream, but although he ran until he fell into a pool, he caught nothing.

Drenched and cold, he wished that he had not been so boastful, but still hoped that he might catch the night, and so again took up his position beside the trap, and when the wind blew up a storm of rain and thunder he called, "Who are you?"

A rift appeared in the clouds and a star shone out, saying, "I am the star that heralds the dawn."

The tired trapper climbed the highest tree, but could not reach the star, or the heavy clouds, or the violent flashes of lightning that darted here and there from the sky, and venturing onto too thin a branch in the rain and darkness he slipped and fell into a thorn bush.

Painfully he untangled himself and turned to his basket trap. As he peered into it in the darkness, it was so dense a black inside that he hurriedly tied it up, saying, "If I can't catch the night in my hand, at least I have got it in my basket." Then, away in the distance he heard the first cock heralding the dawn in the village, and joyously setting out for home he opened his trap in front of his friends by the first rays of the morning sun. To his shame there was nothing but daylight in it, and, as his friends laughed at him, they said, "Another time you will have more wisdom than to boast of that which is impossible."

MOTHER OF THE FOREST

An old woman had become so feeble that her family could get no more work out of her, and they chased her away to die in the forest.

The old woman made herself a little hut, and, being too feeble to garden she lived on the few wild roots and fruits that she was able to gather.

The animals of the forest took pity on her when they saw her sad plight.

"I will adopt her as my mother," said the buffalo.

"So will I," said the leopard and the lion together.

"And so will I," said the elephant. "We will feed her and protect her as long as she lives."

The lightning flashed down from a black cloud in the sky and hissed, "She shall be my mother too."

From now on the old woman was well cared for. She had nothing to do, for her adopted children housed, fed and clothed her.

One morning, just as the first streaks of light appeared in

63

the east, the old mother of the forest heard a terrible rustling in the distance. It became louder and louder until it roared like a hurricane. Looking out of her hut she was horrified to see an enormous bird flying down, with wings so wide that they would cover the village. It dropped to earth quite close to her hut, and its weight made the ground tremble.

"Who are you?" asked the old mother.

"I am the merciless one," replied the bird. "I conquer all. Lions and elephants, crocodiles and hippos—I make them into finger rings. Go and dig your garden at once, or I will kill you."

The poor old mother of the forest took her hoe and set off to dig, but she was soon exhausted, and when the buffalo came to her later in the day, he found her quite worn out.

"Why are you so weak and trembling today?" he asked.

"A terrible bird came and threatened me with death if I did not dig my garden," she answered.

The buffalo became so furious that he cracked the trees with blows from his horns, and vowed vengeance on the bird.

"Tell me when he comes and tomorrow I will wait and kill him."

"He comes just before dawn."

That night the buffalo kept watch in the old woman's hut. Just as the first streaks of light appeared in the east the terrible rustling sounded through the forest, and soon the great bird pounced down outside the hut, making the ground tremble as he alighted.

"Old woman, old woman, come out and hoe your garden," he called. "I am the merciless one. I conquer all. Lions and elephants, crocodiles and hippos—I kill them and make them into finger rings."

"Run out quickly, Mother, or he will kill us both," groaned the buffalo, and as soon as the bird had gone he lumbered off into the forest, thoroughly frightened.

Later in the day the lion and the leopard came to bring their mother meat, and found her trembling with weakness.

"Why are you so weak today?" they asked.

"A terrible bird came and threatened me with death if I did not dig in my garden."

They leaped at the trees, and tore down branches in their fury, growling, "When did he come? For tomorrow we will wait for him and kill him."

"He came just before dawn."

That night the lion and the leopard kept watch in the old woman's hut. Just as the first streaks of light appeared in the east the trees were swept into a hurricane as the great bird swooped down outside the hut, making the ground tremble as he alighted.

"Old woman, old woman, come out and dig your garden," he called. "I am the merciless one. I conquer all. Lions and elephants, crocodiles and hippos—I kill them and wear them as my finger rings."

"Run out quickly and hoe the garden," groaned the lion and the leopard together in fright, "or he will eat us up as easily as he would a mouse."

When the mother of the forest went off feebly with her hoe they slunk away in different directions with their tails between their legs.

Later in the day the elephant came to see his mother and found her thin and weak. On his asking the reason, she told him, "The merciless bird threatened me with death if I did not dig my garden, but, in any case, I am nearly dead."

The elephant flew into such a rage that he knocked down or uprooted all the trees around the old woman's hut.

"I cannot get into your hut," he bellowed, "but I will wait at the back of it. When does he come, for I will kill him tomorrow."

"He comes at the first streak of dawn."

Just as the first streaks of light appeared in the east the

wind blew in gales with the sweep of the great bird's wings, and he alighted just outside the old woman's hut, making the ground tremble.

"Old woman, old woman, come out and dig your garden," he called, "I am the merciless one. Lions and elephants, crocodiles and hippos—I kill them and wear them as my finger rings."

The elephant became so frightened that his skin grew flabby and hung around him in folds. Putting his trunk through the back of the thatch he whispered, "Go out and dig quickly, Mother, or we shall all be killed."

The old woman took her hoe and dragged her limbs wearily to the garden. When the way was clear, the elephant charged into the forest as fast as his legs would carry him.

That afternoon there was a thunderstorm and the lightning came hissing down out of a black cloud to visit his mother. He found her as thin as a finger and nearly dead.

"Mother, why are you so weak today?" he asked.

She answered weakly, "The merciless one came and made me dig my garden under threat of death, but if I have to go out and dig again tomorrow I shall die in any case."

The lightning flew into such a rage that he crashed and roared, burning up all the trees in the neighborhood and smashing the rocks into splinters.

"When does he come?" he asked. "For tomorrow I will be watching, and will kill him however big he may be."

"He comes just before dawn."

Just as the first streaks of light appeared in the east a great black cloud hung over the forest where the old woman had her hut.

Presently a furious hurricane blew from the wings of the great bird. He pounced down outside the old woman's hut, making the ground tremble, and shouted, "Old woman, old woman, come out and hoe your garden."

"I am too weak today," she groaned.

"Then I will peck you to bits," shrieked the bird. "I am the merciless one. I conquer all. Lions and elephants, crocodiles and—" Before he could finish his sentence there was a crack as though the sky would burst, and the lightning flashed down right among the great feathers.

"Bang! Crash!" shrieked the lightning in his rage as he forked and zigzagged, flinging flesh and feathers right across the hills, "I will teach you such a lesson that you will never again victimize our old mother." Then the lightning leaped back into the black cloud in a blinding flame.

The old mother of the forest never had to work any more. Her children were ashamed at the way in which they had deserted her, and all the animals did what they could to make her last days peaceful, while for many weeks there was feasting in the forest where men and beasts were enjoying the flesh of the merciless one.

HOW BABY WART HOG SAVED HIS FATHER'S LIFE

Of all the beasts in the forest, Ntambo the lion was the most treacherous, for he would profess friendship and even descend to flattery, only to pounce upon his victim and devour him.

One day, meeting Penge the wart hog, he called out, "Friend Penge, draw near and let us be friends. Why should you always stay at such a distance from me? I have heard of your skill as a doctor, and you know of my prowess as a

68

hunter. I will agree to feed you, if you, on your part, will promise to heal me when I am sick."

Penge thought to himself, "If he is sick, he is not likely to do me any harm." So he called aloud, "All right, Ntambo, if you are sick I will look after you, but I cannot stop today. I'm in a hurry. Goodbye."

A few days later all the lion cubs were hungry. Ntambo had not caught anything to eat, so he sent one cub around to Penge's hut, asking him to come at once as he was terribly ill.

When Penge heard the message, he prepared to go, but his wife guessed that there was foul play and warned him not to set out.

Baby Penge heard the argument and said, "Father, put me into an earthenware pot. I am so small that nobody will know that I am there. Seal up the mouth of the pot, but leave a little hole for me to breathe. Send the pot to Ntambo saying that you are preparing to visit him, but must first have some of his hair for the medicine, and that he must put it into the hole in the pot. In this way I will be able to hear if he has any evil designs upon you."

Baby Penge was sealed up in the pot and taken to the lion cub, who stood outside the door waiting to carry it to his father, with an appropriate message of sympathy.

When the lion cub reached home he was greeted with a chorus of disappointment from the hungry family. "Why did you not bring us a wart hog for breakfast?"

"He will come very shortly," answered the lion cub. "I have brought a pot of medicine which he is compounding for you. Penge wishes you to add some of your hair to the ingredients and to send it back. Later he will come himself to administer it."

A bunch of Ntambo's mane was pulled out and slipped into the hole at the top of the pot. Poor little baby Penge had great difficulty in stifling his coughs as the hair fell into

69

his nose and his mouth and his eyes.

"Put a pot of water on the fire. I will soon be back with Penge and we shall have a good breakfast," said the lion cub as he set out to take the pot of medicine back to Penge's home. Little did he think that all he was saying had been heard by the baby wart hog inside the pot.

The pot was quickly handed to Mrs. Penge. She took it inside the hut and opened it.

"Father must not go near Ntambo's hut. Their friendship is false, and they already have a pot of water on the fire with which to cook him," said baby Penge as he spat and wiped the lion's hair from his mouth and face.

Naturally, Penge sent a polite message back to Ntambo

saying, "Since you have so good an appetite as to want to eat me, I do not think that you are ill enough to need a doctor."

TEACHING BABY CRAB TO WALK

Nkala the crab was delighted that he had a baby, and hoped that his son would be the most correct and proper crab. Later, however, he was grieved to see little Nkala sidling along instead of walking straight.

"My son," he said, "always remember that you should walk straight forward." But despite all the lessons and talk of his father, baby crab persisted in walking sideways.

For many many days the two might be seen at the bottom of the stream, and each day Father Nkala put more and more energy into teaching his son to walk straight. At last the little fellow became disheartened and said, "Father, just walk straight yourself, and show me how it is done."

The father crab started proudly along the sand at the bottom of the stream, but though he tried hard to walk straight, he had been so accustomed to walking at a slant that nature was too strong for him, and he still went sideways.

The little crab cried out with glee, "If that is all that you want, I can walk like that too, Father," and ever since, the baby crab has grown up walking sideways, which shows how much stronger were his father's actions than his words.

THE TWO BOXES

When the Great Spirit was giving to each creature his work in life he called the black man and the white and set before them two boxes, saying, "These boxes each contain gifts, and each box will show the work for which its owner is best suited."

The Great Spirit loved the black man, and gave him the first choice. The black man saw that one box was very big and heavy and the other box was very small and light, so he chose the heavy box, and struggling till he got it onto his shoulder he staggered home with it and opened it.

Inside were hoes and axes, water pots and forked sticks used for carrying loads. And since then the black man has usually had the work of chopping wood, drawing water, and carrying loads.

The white man was at first very disappointed that he was left with so small and light a box, and even more so when he opened it and found that it only contained a pencil to put behind his ear and a piece of paper to carry in his pocket. But whereas the wisdom of a black man dies with him because there is nobody to write it down, when the white man learns something new he always puts it onto his paper, so that when he dies his paper still remains to show others the wisdom that he has gathered. And so it is that the pencil and books put the white man in advance of the black.

 # THE CHILDREN WHO COULD
DO WITHOUT THEIR ELDERS

In the kingdom of Kibengo, all the children became dissatisfied with the rule of their fathers and mothers.

"Why should we help them to dig the gardens?" they asked. "Why should we obey them, and do all that they command? We are human beings, with as much right to be obeyed as they."

So the children rebelled and were punished. They rebelled again, and were punished again. This continued until the boys and girls determined to kill off all the old people, and to appoint a king of their own.

The plot succeeded well. All the old people were killed excepting two, for one boy loved his father and mother so much that he hid them, and nobody else knew that they were still alive.

The next step was to appoint a king of their own. But even when he was appointed nobody wanted to obey him. All wished to be kings, but nobody wanted to be a servant. Everybody wished to make others work, but nobody wanted to work himself.

In the new kingdom of Kibengo matters went very badly, for none wanted to cook the food, but all wished to eat it. Nobody would sow, or weed the gardens, but all desired to harvest them. When the old people were alive their sons and daughters each thought that he, or she, knew better than their father or mother, but now that all the old people were dead it was surprising how often one might hear the remark, "If Father had only been here he would have shown me," or, "If only Mother were here she would do it for me."

At last, however, by suffering and starvation, the children were forced into some degree of order, and their king became recognized as a king.

Then came a dreadful happening. A huge snake one day wriggled into the royal enclosure, and coiling itself around the king, threatened to kill him. All the boys and girls went running here and there in fright, not knowing what to do, and each accusing the others of doing the wrong thing. If they left the snake, it would kill their king, while if they attacked it, it would merely become enraged and strike him all the sooner.

At the height of the confusion, the boy who had hidden his parents ran off to ask their advice.

His father told him, "My son, a snake can never resist a jumping frog. Run to the stream, fetch a frog, and throw it down near the snake."

A frog was quickly brought and thrown down in front of the snake. At once the snake left the boy king, seized the frog, and the children soon beat the snake to death.

"You have saved my life," the king declared, "but I fancy that such wisdom was that of elders, and not that of a boy. Fetch out your parents and we will enthrone them. We have found how foolish it is for children to try to live without their elders, for we have not the wisdom of experience. Let us have an older person to command us, and let us all obey him."

THE BACHELORS AND THE PYTHON

There were only two unmarried men in the village. All the rest had found suitable partners, but Kalemeleme was so gentle that he would not stand up for his own rights, or anyone else's, while Kinku was so bad-tempered that no one could stand his tantrums for long.

Thus these two lived in unhappy loneliness, until one day Kalemeleme took his bow and arrows and going into the forest in the early morning, when the dew was on the grass, he shot a gray wildcat and a brown wildcat.

On his way home he met Moma, the great rock python, mightiest snake in the forest, and was about to shoot when Moma pleaded, "Gentle one, have mercy on me, for I am stiff with cold. Take me to the river where it is warm."

Touched with pity, Kalemeleme took the great reptile on his shoulders to the stream and threw him in.

Moma lifted his head above the reeds and said, "Thank you, gentle one. I have seen your loneliness. Throw in your gray wildcat and your brown wildcat and take what the water-spirit gives you."

Kalemeleme threw his gray wildcat and his brown wildcat into the river. Immediately the water began to ripple and grow redder and redder until beneath the surface there appeared a great, red, open mouth.

He put in his hand and pulled out a gourd. He took it home and opened it. Out stepped the most beautiful girl

that was ever seen, and she was as good as she was lovely.
She could weave mats, plait baskets, and make pots. She kept
the house so neat, and cultivated the garden so well, she prepared the food so carefully and helped her neighbors so
willingly, that soon Kalemeleme and his beautiful wife were
the favorites of the village.

Kinku came to him and asked, "Tell me, Kalemeleme,
where did you get your wife?"

"The water spirit gave her to me," Kalemeleme replied,
and he told him the circumstances.

"Well, I want a wife too," said Kinku, so he took his bow
and his arrows and went off into the forest when the sun
was boiling hot overhead.

He killed a gray wildcat and a brown wildcat. On his way
home he too met Moma, the mighty python, wilting with

the heat under a bush. He was about to shoot when Moma pleaded, "Mercy, Kinku. Have mercy on me for I am suffocated with this heat. Take me to the river where it's cool."

"What! Take you, a loathsome reptile? Find your own way to the river!"

"Very well. Come along." And the snake glided through the undergrowth, while Kinku followed.

Moma plunged into the water and, lifting his head above the reeds, he called out, "Kinku, I have seen your loneliness. Now throw in your gray wildcat and your brown wildcat and take what the water spirit gives you."

Kinku threw in his gray wildcat and his brown wildcat. At once the water began to ripple and became redder and redder, until beneath the surface Kinku saw a huge open mouth.

He put in his hand and drew out a pumpkin. He staggered home with it. It became heavier and heavier as he went, and at last he dropped it. It cracked, and out stepped the ugliest woman that ever was. Before Kinku could recover from his shock she boxed him soundly on the ears, and taking him by the nose she said, "Come on, Kinku. I am your wife."

She didn't give him the chance to say "no," but pummeled him and pushed him, bullied him and blamed him. She led him a dog's life, for she was as lazy as she was hideous. "Kinku, carry the water! Kinku, cut the firewood! Kinku, cultivate the garden! Kinku, cook the meal!" while she simply lay about and abused him.

Of course Kinku blamed the water spirit, but had he only known it, he had nobody to blame but himself.

THE RABBIT STEALS
THE ELEPHANT'S DINNER

One day Kalulu the rabbit was watching the children of
Soko the monkey playing in the trees, and saw one monkey
reach out his tail and catch his brother around the neck,
holding him a helpless prisoner in mid-air.

Kalulu thought that this was splendid, and although he
had no long tail, he could twist forest creepers into a noose.
During the next few days a number of animals were caught
in this way and held fast in the forest thickets, only escaping
with difficulty. They thought that it was only an accident,
but had they known, it was Kalulu who was experimenting
with his noose.

At last Polo the elephant decided to make a new village,
and, being king of the animals, he called every living thing
in the forest to come and help him build it.

All came with the exception of Kalulu. He had caught a
whiff of the delicious beans which Polo's wives were cooking for his dinner, and when the beans were cold Kalulu
came out of the bushes and ate them up.

Polo was furious when he reached home and found that
his beans had been stolen. Whoever could have taken his
dinner? Next day he told the lion to lie in wait nearby, and
to pounce upon the thief if one appeared. Now Kalulu was
hiding in the bushes and heard the plan, so he spent that

78

night in twisting a big noose, which he set in a side path
close to the cooking pots.

Next morning, when the animals had gone to work on the
new village, Kalulu strolled out into the open and began to
eat Polo's beans, with one eye on the place where he knew
that the lion was hiding. Having finished his meal Kalulu
ran off, when, as he expected, Ntambo the lion leaped out in
pursuit. Kalulu bolted through the noose that he had set,
and when Ntambo followed he was caught and swung into
mid-air, where he wriggled and squirmed till evening, when
the animals returned to the village and set him loose.
Ntambo was too ashamed to admit that he had been fooled

by a little rabbit, so he simply said that some unknown animal had ensnared him.

Next day Mbo the buffalo was set to watch the beans of his chief, but Kalulu had set a great noose between two palm trees. When Kalulu had finished his meal of the chief's beans and was strolling away, the buffalo burst out at him, but the rabbit ran between the two palm trees, and when the buffalo followed he was caught by the noose and swung into mid-air, where he wriggled and squirmed till evening, when the animals returned to set him loose.

Mbo the buffalo was so ashamed that he would not say how he had been outwitted, merely remarking that there must be some rascal dwelling among them.

The leopard, the lynx, the wart hog and the hunting dog were all fooled in the same way, and still Kalulu stole Polo's daily bowl of beans.

At last Nkuvu the tortoise, wiser than the rest, went privately to King Polo the elephant and said, "If your wives will smear me with salt and put me into your dinner of beans tomorrow, I will catch the thief."

Next day Nkuvu was secretly smeared with salt and hidden in the beans. The worthless rabbit again determined to get his dinner without working for it, and having set his noose, he sauntered up to the cooking pots when all the animals were out at work and began to eat. He thought that the beans were even nicer than usual. They were so deliciously salty. But before Kalulu could finish, Nkuvu had bitten tightly onto his foot.

The rabbit screamed, he pleaded, he threatened and offered bribes, but all to no purpose. Nkuvu said nothing, but simply held on to Kalulu's foot, and when the animals returned from the building of the new village Kalulu was still a prisoner.

At once the animals saw who the thief really was, and they determined to pay him back exactly as he had treated them.

For six days he had to do without any dinner, and every day they went off to work leaving Kalulu tied by a noose to a tree. By the time this punishment was finished the rabbit was so thin that the animals took pity on him and let him go, warning him that it was better to work for his food than to steal it, and that although a thief may escape for a time, he will at last surely be caught.

THE RABBIT TAKES HIS REVENGE ON THE ELEPHANT

Kalulu could not forget the punishment that he had received for stealing the elephant's dinner, and he constantly planned his revenge.

At last he noticed that when Polo the elephant submerged himself in the river, he could remain under the water as long as he liked, keeping only his trunk above the surface to breathe in air.

"Polo, I can remain under water longer than you," he challenged.

"I am sure that you can't."

"Then let us try. We will dive in together and will stay under water till sunset."

They both went together to the river, and the rabbit took off his furry jacket and left it in the reeds, while Polo left his heavy coat on the bank.

They plunged in, and a few seconds later Kalulu came up

and saw, as he had suspected, Polo's trunk reaching out above the surface for air.

"Now, Polo," said Kalulu, "I can see that you have planned to cheat me, but I will cheat you instead," and gathering up Polo's heavy skin coat, he took it home for his wife to cook for supper.

About sunset the rabbit returned to the river and dived in, coming to the surface at exactly the same time as Polo.

"You have stayed under just as long as I have," he remarked, "so neither of us has done better than the other. Now let us dress and go home to supper."

The rabbit was soon in his fur, but the elephant went wandering up and down the bank looking for his heavy coat. At last he said, "Someone must have stolen it. I shall be ashamed to go into the village as I am."

"It is getting dark," said Kalulu. "Come and have supper with me first."

The rabbit's wife had prepared broth from Polo's skin, and both enjoyed their supper.

As they separated Kalulu shouted after Polo, "Elephant, you punished me, so now I have punished you by making you eat your own skin."

The elephant was furious, and bellowing out his rage he charged after the rabbit and nearly trampled on him, but just in time Kalulu dived into his burrow.

Polo did not know that this burrow had many exits, and thought to himself, "I will dig out this Kalulu and eat him. That will be a fitting reward for his having made me eat my skin."

Seizing a pointed stick, he began to dig. Kalulu ran along under the ground and coming up at a distance he shouted, "Good evening, Polo! What are you digging for?"

Polo did not know it was the same rabbit and he answered, "I am digging out this bad rabbit, and am determined to eat him for his impudence."

"I will bring my hoe and help you."

They dug and they dug, till presently Kalulu shouted, "Polo, my hoe has come loose from the handle. Please knock it in firmly with your teeth."

Polo bellowed with rage as he broke off one tooth after the other. "Now," he said, "I will kill and eat two rabbits instead of one," but Kalulu again dived down his burrow and escaped.

Presently he came out of another hole and shouted, "Good evening, Polo. What are you digging for?"

Polo did not know that it was the same rabbit and he answered, "I am digging out two bad rabbits and am determined to eat them for their impudence."

"I will bring my axe and help you."

They dug and they dug, till presently Kalulu shouted, "Polo, my axe has come loose from the handle. Please knock it in firmly with your feet."

Polo knocked it in, but he bellowed with rage as he cut his feet one after the other.

"Now," he said, "I will kill and eat three rabbits instead of two," but Kalulu once more dived down his burrow and escaped.

Presently Kalulu came out of another hole and shouted, "Good evening, Polo. Why are you standing there shivering without your jacket?"

"I am digging out three bad rabbits, and am determined to eat them for their impudence."

"I will bring my pick and help you."

Polo did not know that it was the same rabbit. They dug and they dug, till Kalulu shouted, "Polo, my pick has come loose from its handle. Please knock it in for me."

"What should I knock it in with? My teeth are broken, and my feet are wounded."

"You have a splendid forehead. Surely nothing could hurt so fine a head. Knock it in with that."

The elephant was flattered, and knocked the pick a tremendous blow with his forehead. The pick pierced his skull and he fell down dead.

"Serves him right," said the rabbit. "Those who listen to flattery are sure to come to harm. Pride lost you your coat, your teeth, your feet, and now it has cost you your life. Foolish Polo. Why did you not learn your lesson?"

THE RABBIT GROWS
A CROP OF MONEY

When the rainy season began and the chief was arranging the gardening program, he called the animals and asked what each would sow. One chose maize and another millet. One promised to grow kassava and another rice.

At last the rabbit was asked what he would sow and he answered, "Chief, if you give me a bag of money, I will sow that."

"Whoever heard of sowing money?" asked the chief.

"Then I will show you how to do it," answered Kalulu.

When Kalulu received the bag of money, however, he went off and spent it all on clothes, dried fish, beads and other things.

At harvesting time the chief sent word to the rabbit, saying, "Kalulu, bring in the money that you have harvested."

"The money grows very slowly. It is just in the blade," said Kalulu.

The rabbit spent another year in laziness, and when harvest time again came around the chief sent word, saying, "Kalulu, bring in the money that you have harvested."

"The money grows very, very slowly. It is just in flower," answered Kalulu.

Kalulu spent another year of idleness, and when harvest time again arrived the chief sent word, saying, "Kalulu, bring in the money that you have harvested."

"The money grows very slowly," said the rabbit. "It is just in the ear."

The rabbit was now beginning to feel he was on the spot and did not know what to do, for when one tells one lie it generally leads to another.

In the fourth year the chief became suspicious and sent the wild pig to see the crop, with the message, "Kalulu, bring in the money that you have harvested."

Kalulu knew now that he must do something, but he did not know what to do. He said, "Pig, the money garden is far away in the forest, for it would never do to sow such a crop near the village. Everyone would want to steal it."

"Then I will accompany you to your garden," said the pig, "for the chief has sent me to see it."

Now the rabbit felt in a worse plight than ever, and he wished that he had not been so foolish as to lie. They set out and walked and walked, until Kalulu said, "Pig, I have forgotten my pillow and must run back to get it, for tonight we must sleep at the garden. It is now too far to get back in one day."

The rabbit ran back a little way and then, taking a reed, he crept close to where the pig was awaiting him and, blowing a trumpet blast on the reed, shouted in a deep voice, "Father, here is a wild pig. Come quickly and let us kill him."

The pig thought that the hunters were upon his track and ran for his life. Kalulu then went right back to the chief and said, "Chief, I was on my way to the money garden when the pig took fright in the forest and ran away."

85

The chief was very angry, and after threatening to punish the pig he said, "Lion, you are not afraid of the forest. Go with Kalulu, that he may show you his money garden."

Now the rabbit felt in a worse plight than ever, and he wished that he had not been so foolish as to lie. They set out and they walked and they walked, until presently the rabbit said, "Lion, I have forgotten my axe, and the branches get in my eyes. Just wait till I run home for the axe."

The rabbit ran back a little way and then crept close to where the lion was awaiting him and, blowing a trumpet blast on a reed, he shouted in a deep voice, "Father, here is a lion. Bring your arrows and let us shoot him."

The lion was so frightened when he thought that the hunters were upon his track that he ran for his life. Kalulu then went straight to the chief and said, "Chief, I was taking the lion to see the beautiful crop of money that I have grown for you, but he took fright in the forest and ran away."

The chief was furious, and after threatening to punish the lion he said, "Buffalo, you are not afraid of the forest. Go with Kalulu, that he may show you his money garden."

Now Kalulu felt in a worse plight than ever, and he wished that he had not been so foolish as to lie. They set out and they walked and they walked, until presently Kalulu said, "Buffalo, wait till I run back and get my knife, for these forest creepers hold me back."

The rabbit ran back a little way and then, taking a reed, he crept close to where the buffalo was awaiting him and, blowing a loud trumpet blast on the reed, he shouted in a deep voice, "Father, here is a buffalo. Bring your spears and let us kill him."

The buffalo thought that the hunters were upon him and ran for his life. Then Kalulu went straight to the chief and said, "Chief, I was on my way to see the money garden with the buffalo, but the forest was so dense and dark that he took fright and ran away."

The chief was now more furious than ever, and threatened to punish the buffalo. "Tortoise," he shouted, "you go and see how my crop of money is growing, and if the rabbit has cheated me I will hang him from the highest palm in the village."

Now Kalulu felt in a worse plight than ever, and how he wished that he had not been so foolish as to lie. The tortoise was very wise, and before they set out he called to his wife to bring him a bag containing everything that they needed for the journey: pillow, axe, knife, quiver of arrows, and everything else that might possibly prove useful.

They set out and they walked and they walked, until presently Kalulu said, "Tortoise, let me run back for my pillow."

"It's all right," said the tortoise. "You can use mine."

They went on and on, until Kalulu said, "Tortoise, let me run back for my axe."

"Don't worry," said the tortoise. "I have mine here."

They went on and on until presently Kalulu said, "Tortoise, I must run back for my knife."

"It does not matter," said the tortoise. "I have mine here."

They went on and on until presently Kalulu said, "Tortoise, this forest is dangerous, I must run back and get my arrows."

"It's all right," said the tortoise. "I have my arrows here."

The rabbit now felt in a worse plight than ever. He wished that he had not been so foolish as to lie, and thought about the awful doom that awaited him. He could almost feel the rope around his neck, and wondered what the chief would say when the deception was found out. Finally, in his fright, he ran off into the forest and bolted home as fast as his legs could carry him.

"Quick, wife!" he shouted. "We have not a moment to lose. You must pretend that I am your baby. Pull all my fur out, and rub me over with red clay. Then when the chief sends his messenger here, nurse me, and say that there is nobody but the baby in the house with you."

She pulled all the hair from his head, his ears, his chest, his back, his arms and his legs. Oh, how it hurt! Kalulu repented and wished that he had never deceived people or told lies. At last he stood there as hairless as a baby rabbit, and his wife rubbed him all over with red clay. She had hardly finished when a soldier came from the chief, saying, "Where is Kalulu? We have come to take him to be hanged for deceiving the chief and for running away from the tortoise."

"Baby and I are the only rabbits in the house," said Kalulu's wife.

"Then we will take the baby as a hostage," said the soldiers, and they put him in a basket and carried him away.

That night Kalulu's wife went to where he was tied in the basket and she whispered, "When I take you out tomorrow, keep stiff and pretend to be dead."

Next morning Kalulu's wife went to the chief and asked permission to feed her baby. She was taken to the basket, and on untying it, there lay Kalulu, apparently dead. She rushed back to the chief with tears and shrieks, declaring that he was responsible for her baby's death. A great public hearing was called, and all the animals agreed that the chief must pay, so he gave Kalulu's wife the biggest bag of money that he possessed, and told her to take her baby and bury it.

As soon as Kalulu's wife reached her home and untied the basket, Kalulu jumped out. "Oh, how I have suffered," he groaned. "I had to keep stiff though my limbs ached and my toes were cramped in the basket. I will never deceive anyone or tell lies again."

His wife showed him the bag of money, and after waiting till his hair was grown, he set out with it for the chief's village.

"Chief," he said, "I have just returned from my long, long journey to get you the harvest from your money. Here it is. The tortoise was too slow, and I could not wait for him."

The chief took the money and thanked Kalulu for the splendid crop, but was ashamed to tell him of his dead baby. As for the rabbit, he went home very glad that he had managed to get out of the scrape, and vowed that it was the last time he would ever lie.

THE LEOPARD AND THE RABBIT GO COURTING

Kalulu the rabbit and Nge the leopard both heard of the most beautiful girl who ever was, and each determined to woo her for his wife. They set out to court her but met on the way, and as each explained his errand they decided to go together.

When they reached the girl's home, they asked her father what present he desired in exchange for his daughter's hand.

The father saw that he was in a dilemma and must get rid of one or the other of these suitors. So he told the rabbit, "There is only one thing that I desire, and that is a leopard's skin."

"There is no difficulty about getting that," said the rabbit, and at once began to plan to kill the leopard.

The father of the beautiful girl then told the leopard, "There is only one thing that I want of you, and that is a rabbit's skin."

"There is no difficulty about getting that," said the leopard, and at once began to plan to kill the rabbit.

Before they left, the beautiful girl called them both and said, "Whoever marries me must build me a most splendid house. It must be unlike any other person's house. I want rafters of bone and thatch of feathers, for then I shall know that my husband is so skillful a hunter that I shall never starve."

Kalulu and Nge walked home quite a respectable distance apart, in case one should seize and kill the other. Each talked loudly of the ease with which he would get sufficient animals for the rafters of bone, and sufficient birds for the thatch of feathers.

All day long the leopard prowled through the forest, hunting for animals whose bones he could use for rafters, but he only caught one bushbuck.

The rabbit prepared a very big bag with a small hole in the bottom, big enough for him to pass his hand through. Then, going off to the plains, he sat down near a herd of roan antelope and called, "My friends, come into the shade of this tree and I will show you wisdom." Then he placed his bag over a tree root.

The roan antelope approached in a herd and Kalulu said, "Though I am so light, you cannot lift me, and though you are all so heavy, I can lift the whole herd of you together. Is not that very wonderful?"

"We do not believe you," said the antelope.

"Then wait until I get into the bag, and then try to lift me," and Kalulu jumped into the bag. He closed it so that the antelope would not see what he was doing. Then Kalulu put his hand through the hole in the bottom of his bag, took hold of the tree root and shouted, "Lift!" But although first one and then all together tried to lift him, he held tightly to the root and they had to admit that he was too heavy for them.

"That is very remarkable," they all agreed, "but at least you cannot lift us all together, for it takes eight strong men to carry one of us."

"Jump into the bag and let me show you," said Kalulu. But when they were all in the bag Kalulu tied the string, clubbed them to death, and took home their bones to make his rafters.

When Nge the leopard saw how quickly Kalulu had found the bones with which to build his house, he asked how he had been so wonderfully successful.

"It is not wonderful at all," said Kalulu. "You only use your strength, but I use my wits. Tomorrow we will get the feathers for the thatch."

That night Kalulu wove a very big basket, and with this he wandered into the marshes next morning, greeting each of the birds by name.

"What brings you here, Kalulu," they asked, "when you are accustomed to living on the hillside?"

"I am getting so heavy that I have come to seek work."

"What nonsense! You are not heavy."

"Let us try an experiment then," said Kalulu, putting his

basket over the roots of a tree. "If you can lift me, I will give you the fur off my back, while if I can lift you, you must give me the feathers from your wings."

He jumped into the basket and pulled down the lid. Then, pushing his hand through the bottom, he held tightly to the tree roots, and although the birds tried first singly and then all together, they could not lift him, for he had hold of the roots.

"That is very wonderful," they all agreed, "but at least you cannot lift us all together."

The birds now all hopped into the basket: the crane, the pelican, the heron, the stork, the water hen, the diver, and many more. The fishing eagle, the ibis and the kingfisher all flocked into the basket, for they wanted to make it so heavy that the rabbit could not lift it. But the rabbit soon closed the lid and proceeded to pour boiling water over them. Then he plucked their feathers for his thatch.

The only things which now remained to complete Kalulu's preparation for his wedding were the leopard skin and the meat for the feast. For the latter Kalulu determined to try to capture a troop of baboons, so taking his bag he went in search of them. But by this time his trick had become known in the forest, and the baboons guessed, as soon as they saw Kalulu with his bag, that he wished to deceive them in the same way as he had the roan antelope and the water birds, so they closed about him to kill him.

"Ah, you know my trick," said Kalulu, and dropping his bag he fled for his life.

One big baboon shouted after him, "Never mind, Kalulu! Although we cannot catch you now, we know where your beautiful new house is, and we will come and kill you to-night."

Kalulu went back to the spot where Nge and he were to build their houses. "How have you managed with your feathers for the thatch?" asked Kalulu.

"Very badly indeed," answered Nge. "Each time I make a dash at a covey of red-legged partridges or guinea fowl, they fly off, and I never manage to snatch more than a few bedraggled tail feathers."

Kalulu pretended to be most sympathetic. He said, "Nge, your difficulty is that you hunt depending only on your strength. I use my wits. But never mind. I will give you my house."

Never suspecting foul play, the leopard was delighted, and took the house which Kalulu had built of bones and thatched with feathers. That night after the moon had set the baboons planned to take their revenge. Armed with clubs they came to the hut and shouted. Nge came out to see who was there, and the baboons, thinking that it was Kalulu, clubbed him to death before he could recover from his surprise, and left his body outside the hut.

Kalulu was hiding in the forest close by and heard the dying groans of his rival. So next morning he presented himself at the house of his father-in-law with the leopard skin in his hand and carrying a basket of leopard meat for the feast upon his shoulder, and claimed his bride.

HOW THE RABBIT MADE ENEMIES BY TRYING TO BE TOO FRIENDLY

When the bushbuck Gulungu was running for his life from Nge the leopard, the rabbit saw him plunge into the stream and crouch down among the reeds until only his ears and horns could be seen above the water.

The leopard, following upon his trail, came to the water's edge, and thinking that the horns were the branches of a tree he took hold of one and leaned far out over the stream, saying, "Wherever can that bushbuck have gone?"

The rabbit wanted to be friends with both, so he first called, "Bushbuck, don't move or the leopard will detect you," and then, "Leopard, don't let go, or you will have to do without your dinner."

The bushbuck dived and got away and the leopard was sent sprawling into the water, but neither of them appreciated the kindness of Kalulu, for, said the leopard, "Had he not warned the bushbuck, I might have killed and eaten him," and, said the bushbuck, "He cannot have cared for me, or he would not have told the leopard to keep hold of me."

Thus when Kalulu tried to please both sides, he ended by pleasing neither.

THE TORTOISE AND THE REEDBUCK RUN A RACE

Tolwe the reedbuck was one day boasting of his speed when the tortoise laughed at him in disdain.

"Why are you laughing?" asked Tolwe.

"Because you are so slow," said Nkuvu the tortoise. "I can race you and leave you behind."

A big argument followed and at length it was agreed that next day they should race twenty miles to a certain village.

"When you have reached the first village," said Nkuvu,

"shout and I will answer you. At the second shout again and I will answer you. At the third shout and I will answer you again, and at the last you will find me awaiting you. You run along the path, but I am accustomed to the grass, and will run through the forest."

All the animals laughed and thought that Nkuvu had no chance. Now Nkuvu had four brothers, so alike that nobody could tell one from the other. He said to them, "I want you all to help me to win this race. One must wait at the first village, and when Tolwe shouts, must answer, "Come along! I have been waiting for you." Another must do the same at the second village, another at the third, and the last must await Tolwe at the end of the road, and greet him as he arrives."

All the animals were astir early in the village, and at sunrise the tortoise and the reedbuck set out, the tortoise strolling leisurely into the grass, where he fell asleep, and the reedbuck trotting lightly along the road, with the thought that he had already left his rival far behind. He was shocked, however, when at the first village he found a tortoise standing in the path.

"Come, come," said the tortoise. "If you wish to race me you must make better speed than that, or I cannot waste time in waiting for you."

The sun was now well up, and the reedbuck fled down the path at high speed, so that the perspiration streamed from his sides long before he had reached the second village. But to his dismay the tortoise was standing there quite cool and comfortable.

"Why don't you run?" said the tortoise. "You boasted of your speed, Tolwe, but I am tired of standing here."

Tolwe was already tired with his exertion, but he flew along the path at such speed that his feet scarcely touched the ground. His eyes were bloodshot. Foam was on his chest. His hoofs were bleeding and his flanks heaved, so that by

the time he reached the third village he was giddy and stag-
gering. "Nkuvu!" he shouted.

"Why, Tolwe, you have arrived at last," said the tortoise,
strolling out of the long grass. "I have been having a nap
while I waited for you. Come on! Let us be going."

But the reedbuck was in no condition to continue the
race. He fell to the ground, groaning. "How foolish I was to
boast of my speed. Even a tortoise can outstrip me."

When next the tortoises were together they all agreed that

though they were easy to overcome singly, when they all worked together they were hard to beat.

BUYA MARRIES THE TORTOISE

Moma the huge rock python lived in a hole in the side of the hill. His daughter was the most beautiful creature that had ever been seen. All the animals of the forest loved her, but they were afraid of her father.

At last the elephant decided, "I will ask Moma if I can have his beautiful daughter. I am not afraid. I can strike with my tusks, strangle with my trunk or crush with my feet."

So Polo the elephant coughed outside Moma's hole to announce his presence, and called, "How-d'you-do, Moma!"

"Who are you?" asked the snake as he put his head out of the hole.

Oh! You should have seen those great, glaring, glassy eyes. They were cruel.

The elephant's skin shrank into folds with sheer fright. He held his ground for just a few seconds, then dashed away into the forest.

That evening when the animals came out to play in the village street, the elephant came shambling sadly home.

"Ha-ha!" laughed Ntambo the lion. "You are a coward. Now it's my turn. I'm not scared. I tear with my teeth and rip with my claws. I'll go and ask the python for his daughter."

Next morning the lion coughed outside the snake's hole. "How-d'you-do, Moma!"

"Who are you?" hissed the snake as his head appeared. You should have seen his horrible mouth!

The lion was so scared that he could not answer, but put his tail between his legs and slunk away like a whipped dog.

That evening as the animals came out to dance in the village street, there came the lion with head down, too sad even to answer their greeting.

"Well, well!" snorted the buffalo. "To think that you, the great Ntambo, lion of the forest, were afraid! Now it's my turn. What should I fear? I stamp with my hooves and toss with my horns. I will go and ask Moma for his daughter."

Next morning the buffalo coughed before the entrance to the python's home, calling his greeting, "How-d'you-do, Moma!"

"Who are you?" called the snake as he came out. You should have seen his terrible teeth and his tongue darting in and out!

The buffalo was so startled that he flung up his tail, put down his head, and dashed away into the forest.

That evening, as the animals came out to play in the village street, the buffalo came disconsolately home, so sad that he could hardly put one hoof before another.

The crocodile tried. The hippopotamus tried. The hyena tried. The leopard tried. They all tried, but with the same invariable failure, until none dared even to mention the name of Buya, the beautiful creature that was Moma's daughter.

Then the little tortoise Nkuvu announced, "I have decided to ask Moma for his beautiful daughter in marriage."

"You? You little silly! As if you had a chance when even the elephant has failed!"

"We shall see," was all that the tortoise replied, and going off to the python's hole he coughed as the others had done. "How-d'you-do, Moma!"

99

"Who are you? What do you want?" said Moma, unwinding himself from his hole. You should have seen his head. It was as big as a house, but that was nothing compared to the body that followed it.

"I am Nkuvu the tortoise, and I have come to ask for the hand of Buya, your beautiful daughter, in marriage."

"What! You? I'll crush you!" and the snake wound himself, vast coil on mighty coil, upon the back of the poor little tortoise.

Nkuvu opened his front door. He put in his head. He put in his legs. He shut the door and down he went into the ground under the immense weight of the snake.

"Now he's dead," thought Moma, and uncoiled himself; but Nkuvu was not dead. He just gave a wriggle and came out of his shell. Then, beaming up into the snake's face, he said, "How charming of you to embrace me like that. I'm sure that we shall get on well together."

"What! I can't crush him!" thought the snake. "Then I'll crack him!" and taking the tortoise in his teeth, he flung him into the air till he looked like a little spot in the sky.

The tortoise opened his front door. He put in his head, he put in his legs, and he shut the door. Then he came down and hit the ground with a thump. Nkuvu came out of his shell, and smiling up at the python said, "How kind of you to give me a ride like that. I can see that we shall get on together famously."

"What!" mused the snake. "I can't crush him! I can't crack him! I'll drown him," and he threw the little tortoise far out into the lake.

The tortoise opened his front door. He put in his head. He put in his legs. He shut the door and down he went with a splash into the water. Then, after swimming about for a while in the sunlight, he returned to the bank, beamed up into the python's face and said, "How good of you to give me such a splendid swim. I can see that we shall be the greatest friends."

"What!" pondered the bewildered python. "I can't crush him! I can't crack him! I can't drown him! I know what I'll do. I'll swallow him!" and he opened his great jaws and swallowed the little tortoise in one gulp.

Poor Nkuvu opened his front door. He put in his head. He put in his legs. He shut the door, and down, down, down he went inside the snake.

However, Moma the python had never had such an experience before. He could hear a voice down in the depths of his anatomy chuckling, "Isn't it nice down here! I like this." And Moma was so upset that . . . that . . . well, he did what the whale did with Jonah, and there stood the tortoise before him, declaring, "How much you must like me! I'm sure that you will make a splendid father-in-law."

The snake was nonplussed. He scratched his head with the point of his tail, for it was all he had to scratch it with. He mused, "What am I to do? I can't crush him! I can't crack him! I can't drown him! I can't swallow him! Then all that remains is to give him my daughter in marriage."

And so it happened that that afternoon, as the animals were singing and dancing in the village street, who should come marching up the road but Nkuvu the tortoise, arm in arm with Buya, the python's beautiful daughter.

WHY THE SENDJI RAT HAS NO TAIL

When the Great Spirit was making his gifts to the animals, he began with the nose and ended with the tail. The elephant pushed his way through the forest and got there first, so he received the finest nose, and he can use it as a hand as well.

At last all the animals had received their legs, their hoofs, their fur, and their feathers, each according to his needs, and the Great Spirit called for a big box of tails to be brought. He gave the zebra and buffalo fine tails with which to switch off the flies. He gave the monkeys and baboons tails with which to climb, and long furry tails to the stoat and the squirrel to help them balance themselves. All the animals received tails except for Sendji the big rat. He had found a fine piece of manioc root, and when they called him he answered, "There's plenty of time. Wait until I have finished eating my manioc."

When, however, he had eaten his manioc, the Great Spirit had put back the spare tails and closed the box, and so to this day the sendji rat has had to do without a tail, because he did not come when he was called.

THE COURTING OF THE BAT, THE SPIDER AND THE BEETLE

Kibembe the bat, Tanda Bumbidi the spider, and Nkobwe the beetle were all in love, and could talk of nothing else but the charm of their loves, and their chances of winning a bride.

"My lady-love is the daughter of a blacksmith," said Kibembe the bat, "and since my call is just like the rings of a hammer on the anvil, I know that they will welcome me into the family."

"My lady-love is fond of soft clothing," said Tanda the

spider, "and who should be more welcome than I, who weave a silky web?"

Though Nkobwe the beetle had nothing to commend him but his ample size, he too felt equally sure of winning a bride. Since they were all in the same condition, they determined to set out together to visit their various brides-to-be, but on the road each could only talk and think of his own case, and was annoyed by the persistent chatter of the others.

First they visited the blacksmith's home, and while Kibembe was enjoying the company of his lady-love, Tanda and Nkobwe hid the blacksmith's hammer, saying, "We are tired of his constant chatter all night long, when respectable people want to be asleep, and if we can spoil his chances we will do so."

Next day the blacksmith was furious and wanted to know who had stolen his hammer.

"Why!" said his wife, "it must have been Kibembe, for I heard his ring-ring-ringing call all night long," and the bat was dismissed in disgrace as a thief.

They then visited the intended wife of Tanda the spider, and as he sat chatting with her, Kibembe and Nkobwe put a fish net across her mother's door. In the morning when she came out she was ensnared by it, and worked herself into a fury with her struggles, until it became difficult to set her free.

"Who could have taken such liberties? Of course it is as plain as day. The offender is Tanda, the weaver of nets," and so the spider was sent off in disgrace.

Finally they visited the home of Nkobwe's lady-love, and as he sat chatting with her, Kibembe and Tanda drank a bowl of fruit syrup which she had just made.

When the theft was discovered next morning and the thief was sought, Kibembe and Tanda both said, "However could you suspect us? We are too thin to have drunk so much syrup. It must have been Nkobwe."

Of course Nkobwe was accused and sent off in disgrace, as his ample size would accommodate ten times as much syrup.

On the way home all were so sad and quarrelsome that they finally told on each other, and so the whole plot came to light, after which each determined that next time he went courting he would go alone, and you will be well advised to do the same.

THREE UNSCRUPULOUS MEN

Three rascals set out together to trade. Ngoi, Ilunga and Banze. On the path they found a neat little parcel. As nobody was in sight, they seized the parcel and opened it. It contained three mpunduji, which are rare colored beads, the size of a pigeon's egg. "We can have one each," they all remarked, but each began to think out a plan to keep all three beads for himself. Meanwhile, they wrapped the beads once more in the parcel.

They said, "We are hungry," so Banze agreed to go to the village to buy food. While he was away, Ngoi and Ilunga planned to jump on him when he returned and stab him to death so that they might take his bead. Banze, however, had his own plan. He mixed poison in their food in order to kill them so that he might take *their* beads.

When Banze set down the food which he brought from the village, Ngoi and Ilunga stabbed him in the back and he fell dead. Throwing his body into the forest, they sat down to eat, but were soon convulsed with pain and staggered into the forest, where they too died. In this way all three rascals perished, and the little parcel of beads still lay unclaimed on the path.

SHINGA-MAMBO

When Shinga-Mambo's father was dying, he told his son, "There is nobody who will want to inherit your mother, for she is old. Look after her. Also, son, remember that it is your duty to submit to those who are in positions of authority. Even though you consider them unjust, obey!"

In the years that followed, poor Shinga-Mambo often had cause to remember his father's dying words. He and his widowed mother lived on the outskirts of the village, where the son made a living for the two of them by his skillful hunting. On his return from the forest he had to pass the hut of old counselor Makomwa-meso, who always came out to meet him and ordered, "Throw down a piece of your meat here at the back of my house. Am I not a village elder! Have I not a right to a portion of everything you catch?"

Shinga-Mambo's mother would complain bitterly, "Son, why do you always bring home half a hare, or a bushbuck with only three legs, or ten partridge eggs, when everyone knows that they lay twenty?"

Her son would reply, "Mother, Makomwa-meso has ordered me to throw down a part of my game every time I pass his hut. He has no mercy for a widow or an orphan, so I must obey. You will see. Father was right, and I shall be glad that I have obeyed."

One day Shinga-Mambo killed a bushbuck, and as usual Makomwa-meso made him cut off a leg and leave it behind his hut. He told his mother, in order to allay her indignation, "Mother, it is unjust of Makomwa-meso, I know, but some day we shall be glad that we have taken Father's advice and submitted to him."

That night, a hyena seized the child of the great chief and carried him off, but on passing the hut of Shinga-Mambo he smelled bushbuck meat, and dropping the dead child he carried off the bushbuck instead.

Early in the morning Shinga-Mambo went to cut up the bushbuck meat and was shocked to find it gone and a dead child in its place, while the paw marks of the hyena told him what had happened.

"Mother," he said, "we shall be blamed for this death. Wrap up the dead child in grass and place it in a basket. It is still early, and old Makomwa-meso will not be up. He told me to leave meat at his hut every time that I had a successful hunt."

Silently Shinga-Mambo left the basket containing the dead baby behind Makomwa-meso's hut and crept away.

When Makomwa-meso awoke and came out of his hut he called to his wives, "Look! The orphan boy has left me a basketful of meat. Put it on the rack in the top of the hut."

Presently the wives, counselors and soldiers of the chief were sent far and near to seek for the missing child. When some of them arrived at Makomwa-meso's hut, they said, "Old man, we smell meat. Share it out with us." The basket was brought down, and to everyone's horror the dead child was revealed.

Naturally Makomwa-meso made excuses, saying that he had not known what was in the basket, but nobody believed him, and so the heartless old man was taken to prison and finally executed for his supposed crime.

When the widow and orphan heard of it, they remarked to each other, "How glad we are that we took Father's advice and did not resist even the unjust demands of Makomwa-meso. Now he has been punished and we are free."

A HUSBAND FOR THE CHIEF'S DAUGHTER

She was the most beautiful girl in all the world and her father, the chief, was so proud of her that nobody dared to ask for her hand in marriage. At last the old man felt that he must do something to get her off his hands. However, she was a self-willed young woman, not easily persuaded.

The chief finally hit on a plan. He sent her up a ladder into a great mpafu tree and had the ladder removed. He then announced, "The man who can fetch her down can marry her, but he who fails must be sold as a slave." Many tried, each with his own particular style of allurement, but to no avail.

One came to the foot of the tree immaculately arrayed: omanda shells at his neck, circlets of punduji beads about his waist, his hair braided and oiled, with a cluster of nduba feathers on his forehead as evidence of his prowess on the battlefield. But she would not look at him. She merely said, "I don't like a fop. You would look better as a slave."

Another came with a row of relatives behind him carrying bags of wealth, guns and powder, blankets and gaudy colored cloths, but she only showed a mild interest, remarking, "My father has more wealth than all you can display, why should I leave him for you? You'd do better as a slave."

Young men stood at the foot of the tree and made beautiful orations. Others brought musical instruments and sang enthralling songs, but she mocked them all, saying, "My pet mongoose and lemur can make a better noise than that. Go away and do some useful work as slaves."

One man came striding around the tree, the very impersonation of grace and strength. He was tall and broad, his muscles rippled with health, his eyes flashed and his brow was noble. Surely he was a fit husband for the chief's daughter. Indeed, her eyes followed his movements for quite a time. Then she remarked, "He is so superb, so striking, that were we to marry, all eyes would be on him and I should be a mere nobody in the background." So he was led away with the rest.

Things certainly looked unpromising. The girl had been put up in the tree for three successive days and no one else dared risk his freedom to claim her.

Eventually a young man, Mudyumuke, arrived near the foot of the mpafu tree with a dog and a goat, a basketful of meat and a basketful of sweet potato shoots. He took no notice of the girl up there so that nobody would accuse him of making love to her, or order him to be taken away as a slave. Calling the dog, the young man gave it the potato shoots, and gave the meat to the goat.

The lady in the tree called down to him, "Silly! Goats do not eat meat nor do dogs care for sweet potato shoots. Give the meat to the dog and the sweet potato shoots to the goat."

At first he took no notice of her, so she came lower down the tree to repeat her remarks.

"What did you say?" called the young man. "Come lower so that I can hear you," and he continued giving the dog the sweet potato shoots and the goat the meat.

Now she was quite low down in the mpafu tree and again said, "Mudyumuke, don't be foolish! Give the meat to the dog and the sweet potato shoots to the goat."

"Come and show me how," said Mudyumuke, holding up his arms. She jumped into them, and for all I know she has been in his arms ever since.

"You see," she told her mother, "Mudyumuke was not above being shown. He didn't think himself wiser than I. He and I will not be master and mastered, but we will live our lives together in mutual respect."

Neither you nor I, nor the beautiful girl, however, are so foolish as to imagine that Mudyumuke really did not know which foods were suitable for dogs and goats. Rather, he was wise enough to win first the girl's interest, next her co-operation, and finally her heart.

THE SMALL RED FEATHER

They were always poor and hungry. She would eke out a miserable existence by digging up wild sweet potatoes with a pointed stick, while he would roam the forest looking for a tortoise, a long-nosed rat, or some such delicacy.

One day as he tramped through the forest, wet with dew, scratched by the thorns, entangled in the creepers, dispirited and complaining to himself, he heard a sweet trilling sound from a branch above him.

"Come near and let me tell you something that will help you."

He approached, and a little bird unlike any that he had seen before let drop a small red feather, saying, "I have seen your constant search for food. Take that feather home and cook it. You will be surprised at the result. Then come back tomorrow and I will give you another."

"Silly!" remarked his wife, when he reached his hut and dropped the feather into a pot of boiling water. "I think

hunger has turned your head. Who ever heard of trying to satisfy one's craving with a feather. You might at least have brought the bird."

He did not answer, but his eyes grew wide with amazement. The feather had swollen into a delicious mush, complete with greens and meat and oil.

Every day he went into the forest and every day the small bird let drop a small red feather, which provided so much food that both man and wife became robust and sleek.

Every day she asked, "Who gave you that feather?"

To which he would reply, "Though he is our friend, yet only I may see him. He is a shy little bird who comes when I am alone."

She became jealous and suspicious, often remarking, "If we had the bird instead of the little red feather, then we could have as much food as we wanted all the time."

So she took a stick and secretly followed her husband into the tangled undergrowth. Presently they heard a sweet trilling sound and the little bird flew down with a small red feather in its beak. Before her husband could stop her, his wife struck down their tiny benefactor and, picking it up dead, she said, "Now I need no longer go searching for edible roots, and your days of roaming the forest are over."

However, when she put one of the bird's feathers into a pot of boiling water it remained just a feather. She cooked it all day. At sunset she brought in more firewood and cooked the feather all night, yet it was still only a pathetic little feather reminding her of her cruelty and greed. And so she and her husband slowly starved to death, whereas if they had only been grateful for the kindness they had received, they might still be well and strong.

111

THE INSEPARABLE FRIENDS

It was at the time when the chieftainship was at Lubinda. A great serpent glided slowly up the Saboi Valley devouring whole villages as it came. No, not just a python like that which swallowed Mwabi's two pigs at once. This reptile had a mouth as big as Kunda Cave. It did not bother to take the victims out of their villages, but swallowed the people with their huts and palms, indeed a whole village at a gulp. Kabanga had disappeared and Madimba. At Kalembe two men escaped by climbing Lukwe Hill and hiding among the rocks.

At the same time there was scandal at the court. The chief's only son had made firm friends with the son of a slave. Of course the counselors were indignant. Something had to be done to alienate them from each other's affections, for the young princeling should have selected his friends from among the sons of the aristocracy.

They advised the chief to take out one of the young slave's eyes, so that he should prove unattractive to his friend. No sooner done, however, than the chief's son went to his father and said, "Take out one of my eyes too. I refuse to remain whole while my friend is disfigured."

The chief refused, for he said, "No man with an eye missing can become a chief and you are my heir."

The young man then went to his mother and said, "If

they don't take out my eye as they have done with my friend, then I shall die of grief, or I shall commit suicide."

The counselors saw a chance for their sons to reach the position of the chieftainship, so they all advised, "Take out his eye to save his life," and this was done. The result was, the two one-eyed young men were as close friends as ever.

"What can we do to separate them?" groaned the chief.

"Break the young slave's arm," they replied. So he was kidnapped and taken off into the forest, where his arm was broken by men disguised behind antelope skin masks.

"Now you must break my arm, Father," demanded the chief's son.

"I would not think of it," replied his father, but the young man went to his mother and said, "Mother, I am plaiting a cord with which to hang myself in the forest, unless they break my arm as they have broken my friend's."

So they broke his arm to prevent him committing suicide. After that the prince and the slave were greater friends than ever.

"What can we do to separate them?" wept the chief.

There was a very beautiful girl in the village. Indeed her dazzling charm was such that everyone wanted to marry her. When she heard of the chief's predicament she said, "I know how to separate them. I will make them jealous of each other."

"If you can do it my son shall marry you," declared the chief.

She went and lay on a mat in the shade of a veranda before one of the huts, and when the young men were passing she beckoned the slave to her.

"What do you want?" he asked.

She just giggled and muttered something incoherent.

"Tell me why you beckoned me," he said.

Again she just mumbled.

"I have no time for that nonsense," he said, and left her to join his companion.

"What did she say to you?" asked the young prince.

"She just muttered incoherently," replied the slave's son.

"That's a nice tale! Why do you hide from me what she said? I never kept a secret from you," and the argument became so bitter that the young men separated and vowed that their pact of friendship was at an end.

It certainly looked as though the scheme of the beautiful girl had been a success. Each young man went unhappily home, and as for the girl, neither would look in her direction. They longed for the old sweet days. At last the chief's son took a large sharp knife in his belt, and said he was going down the valley either to kill or to be killed by the huge serpent.

As he approached Lukwe Hill the two men who had managed to escape from the serpent shouted from their hiding place, "Go no farther! The serpent will certainly devour you."

However, the chief's son called back, "That is what I want. I have no wish to live."

Proceeding down the valley, a turn in the path brought him face to face with the snake, its great mouth open as wide as Kunda Cave.

He did not wait to be snapped up but walked right in between the gaping jaws.

Meanwhile, the slave's son was so miserable that he took a long sharp knife in his belt and declared that he was going down into the valley, either to kill or to be killed by the mighty reptile that was ravaging their villages.

As he approached Lukwe Hill, the two refugees called from the rocks, "Friend, go no farther or you will certainly be swallowed up by the great serpent."

The slave called back, "That is just what I want," and continued down the valley until he came face to face with

114

the terrible snake, its mouth agape like Kunda Cave. Before the snake could move he walked right in, and into the arms of his old friend. Of course the quarrel was forgotten. They embraced each other and advanced into the body of the monster. They found the villagers still alive but longing to get out, though that seemed impossible, for every time they made a dash towards its mouth the snake gave a gulp which flung them back.

"We must kill him," declared the friends. "At least we have one arm apiece and with plenty of hard work we should be able to cut out his liver." They searched all over the snake but could not decide which was his liver. However, they found the place that seemed the easiest to cut. First one hacked. When he was tired the other hacked, while the snake rolled and squirmed until it could do so no longer. The villagers begged the young men to stop, for they were being flung from end to end and side to side of the monster's interior. But at last it was dead and the prisoners trooped out of its mouth, wild with joy.

"You have saved us, you have saved us," they shouted and went in a body to the chief. He, poor old man, was so ashamed of himself for having acted so brutally that he said that the heroes must both be chiefs and he would pay them tribute.

The counselors objected, "But nobody can be chief who has a disabled arm or an eye missing," for they had hoped a chief might be chosen from among their own sons. However, the old man waived aside their objections by saying, "Never mind. They have two eyes and two arms between them. Their friendship has triumphed and they must reign together."

It was thus that the chief's son and the slave's son ruled the kingdom together, and everybody loved and respected them since they had delivered their subjects from the horrible snake. But of one thing you may be sure. Neither of

them would consider for a moment marrying the wily beauty
who had so nearly separated them.

THE FRIENDSHIP OF THE TORTOISE
AND THE EAGLE

It was not often that the tortoise and the eagle met, for the
one spent his days in the clouds and the other in the under-
brush. However, when the eagle heard what a warm-hearted
little fellow the tortoise was, he went to pay a call on him.

The tortoise family showed such pleasure in his company
and fed him so lavishly that the eagle returned again and
again, while every time as he flew away he laughed, "Ha, ha!
I can enjoy the hospitality of the tortoise on the ground but
he can never reach my eyrie in the treetop!"

The eagle's frequent visits, his selfishness and ingratitude
became the talk of the forest animals.

The eagle and the frog were never on speaking terms, for
the eagle was accustomed to swooping down to carry a frog
home for supper.

So the frog called from the stream bank, "Friend tortoise,
give me beans and I will give you wisdom." After enjoying
the bowl of beans the frog said, "Friend tortoise, the eagle
is abusing your kindness, for after every visit he flies away
laughing, 'Ha ha! I can enjoy the hospitality of the tortoise
on the ground but he can never enjoy mine, for my eyrie
is in the treetops.' Next time the eagle visits you, say, 'Give
me a gourd, and I will send food to your wife and children too'."

The eagle brought a gourd, enjoyed a feast, and as he left he called back, "I will call later for the present for my wife."

The eagle flew away laughing to himself as usual, "Ha ha! I have enjoyed the tortoise's food, but he can never come to my eyrie to taste of mine."

The frog arrived and said, "Now, tortoise, get into the gourd. Your wife will cover you over with fresh food and the eagle will carry you to his home in the treetops."

Presently the eagle returned. The tortoise's wife told him, "My husband is away but he left this gourd filled with food for your family."

The eagle flew away with the gourd, little suspecting that the tortoise was inside.

The tortoise could hear every word as he laughed, "Ha! ha! I share the tortoise's food but he can never visit my eyrie to share mine."

As the gourd was emptied out onto the eagle's eyrie, the tortoise crawled from it and said, "Friend eagle, you have so often visited my home that I thought it would be nice to enjoy the hospitality of yours."

The eagle was furious. "I will peck the flesh from your bones," he said. But he only hurt his beak against the tortoise's hard back.

"I see what sort of friendship you offer me," said the tortoise, "when you threaten to tear me limb from limb." He continued, "Under the circumstances, please take me home, for our pact of friendship is at an end."

"Take you home, indeed!" shrieked the eagle. "I will fling you to the ground and you will be smashed to bits in your fall."

The tortoise bit hold of the eagle's leg.

"Let me go, let go of my leg, let go of my leg," groaned the great bird.

"I will gladly do so when you set me down at my own home," said the tortoise, and he tightened his hold on the eagle's leg.

The eagle flew high into the clouds and darted down with the speed of an arrow. He shook his leg. He turned and twirled, but it was to no purpose. He could not rid himself of the tortoise until he set him down safely in his own home.

As the eagle flew away the tortoise called after him, "Friendship requires the contribution of two parties. I welcome you and you welcome me. Since, however, you have chosen to make a mockery of it, laughing at me for my hospitality, you need not call again."

TWO HUNTERS

Two men went hunting. One had his sight, but the other was blind, so of course the man who could see went in front, remarking, "You'll be of no use in hunting, but you may help to carry in the meat."

The one who could see stepped over a porcupine quill on the path but it stuck in the blind man's foot. He pulled it out and put it in his quiver, remarking, "One can never tell when such things may prove useful."

The one who could see stepped over a tortoise, but the blind man stepped on it, and, picking it up, he put it in his quiver.

The one who could see did not notice an elephant tusk on the path. He thought it was a fallen branch, but the blind man, with his sense of feeling more keenly developed, realized what it was as soon as he stepped on it, and, picking it up, he put it in his quiver.

Someone had dropped a gun and the one who could see

did not notice what it was among the fallen leaves, but the blind man knew it for a gun as soon as his toes touched it. Picking it up, he put it into his quiver.

Presently it started to rain, and finding a hut in the forest they took shelter, not realizing that it was the home of the lion family.

The lion's wife was at home. "You must not come in here," she said. "You might be eaten. You've made a mistake and come to the wrong house." The man who could see trembled but the blind man sat down unperturbed.

When the lion returned he stood outside the door and said, "Who is in my house? I am the strong one. Look at my mane." And he pushed some through the crack in the door.

"What poor weak stuff!" said the blind man, feeling the lion's mane. "Look at my hair," and he stuck a porcupine quill through the crack.

The lion said, "Then you're strong. Show me what ticks feed on you. These are the ticks that worry me," and pulling one from his ear he handed it around the door.

"What silly little things!" said the blind man. "These are the ticks that hang onto my ears," and he handed the tortoise around the door.

"But I can bite—look at my teeth," said the lion, snarling around the door.

"Look at mine," said the blind man, and he poked the elephant tusk around the door, not letting the lion know that he was unable to see the teeth.

The lion was now trembling with fright, but he said, "Listen to me roar." And he let out an ear-shattering blast.

"Is that all you can do?" said the blind man. "What a funny little noise. Put your ear around the door and hear me roar."

The lion put his ear around the door. The blind man poked the gun into the lion's ear and pulled the trigger.

There was a terrific report and that was the last sound that the lion ever did hear, for he fell dead.

"Now the lion's wife is mine," said the blind man.

"No, she's mine," said the man who could see, and he hit the blind man so hard over the head that his sight came back.

"You hit me first, now it is my turn," said the one who had been blind. Taking the elephant's tusk, he hit his companion over the head so hard that he fell down dead. After that he took the lion's wife home for his own.

THE LEOPARD BUILDS A HOUSE FOR THE BUSHBUCK

"I want a big house, a wide house, a massive house, a house with plenty of rooms," is what the bushbuck told his wife.

"But how will you lift the heavy beams? You are only a little animal. How will you reach the ridgepole? How will you carry in the thatching grass?"

"I can't do that. I will get the leopard to do it."

"How can you get the leopard to build your house?"

"You'll see." And the bushbuck visited the leopard as though just on a friendly call.

"Your house is looking shabby," said the bushbuck. "It's nearly as tumble-down as mine, but I'm planning to build a new one."

"Where do you plan to build?"

"Beyond the spring, where there are plenty of trees."

"You'll be lonely there," mused the leopard, already licking his lips at the thought of a feast.

"I have been hoping that someone will come and build near me, or even share a house with me."

It was thus that the leopard and the bushbuck decided to build a house together, a big house, a wide house, a massive house, a house with plenty of rooms, so that the leopard family could live at one side of it and the bushbuck at the other.

"I will start hoeing the ground, leopard, while you bring in the poles," said the bushbuck, but the leopard did not realize that he was being given the heaviest job.

"Now I'll get the bark rope while you fetch the thatching grass. That's fine!" encouraged the bushbuck, and when that was done, "Now if I dig the holes, you can put in the upright posts."

Soon the house was taking shape. "If you lift the beams into place, I will stand at a distance to tell you when they are straight." Those mighty beams took some lifting, but the bushbuck kept up a stream of encouraging comment. "Splendid! My, how strong you are!"

"If I hand up the withes you can tie them in place," continued the bushbuck. "After that I will soak the bark rope for you to tie the thatch on."

"Now if your wife carries the water to that anthill, you can stamp out the clay and my wife will bring it to the house for me to smear into the walls."

In this way the house was quickly finished, a big white house, a wide house, a massive house, a house with plenty of rooms.

On one side of the house the leopard family was in council: "If we can only get rid of the bushbuck family, the house will be ours, a big house, a wide house, a massive house, a house with plenty of rooms." On the other side of the house the bushbuck family was in consultation: "If we can only get rid of the leopard family, scare them away, the house will be ours, a big house, a wide house, a massive house, a house with plenty of rooms."

From that time onward there was one fatality after another around the new house. The leopard cubs would come in apparently full of regrets, bringing with them one dead bushbuck kid after another. "After all, Mother, it was an accident, we couldn't help it. We were just playing." But the dead bushbuck kids went into the leopard's cook pot all the same.

Mrs. Bushbuck was frantic. "You'll have to do something about it," she kept telling her husband, but although he visited his pit traps day after day, he had never caught anything in them.

At last the happy day arrived when he found a leopard in his trap. He killed and skinned it, striding home with the leopard skin draped ostentatiously over his shoulder. "Look!" he shouted, "I've killed three today. I left the other two to skin tomorrow."

There was consternation in the leopard home. Sometimes the bushbuck would come home once, sometimes twice or three times a day with a leopard skin over his shoulder. The leopard did not realize that each time it was the same skin.

Mrs. Bushbuck confided casually in Mrs. Leopard, "My husband is a clever leopard hunter. He has decided to kill off all the leopards in this piece of forest. Look what a beautiful skin he has brought in today."

The leopard family did not stop to look, however. They left the neighborhood as fast as their legs could carry them.

Now the bushbuck family have the house all to themselves —a big house, a wide house, a massive house, a house with plenty of rooms. The bushbuck tells all his friends that the leopard built it for him.

THE BLACKSMITH LION
AND THE CONCEITED GOAT

The lion had a smithy where he sharpened and repaired the garden implements of all the other animals.

When they brought him their axes or hoes they paid him the utmost deference, with the exception of the goat. This cheeky animal used to say, "Do it at once, Lion, for I am in a hurry. You can leave the work of the other animals until you have finished mine."

For a long time the lion endured this, for he said to his lioness, "I only have claws and teeth, but the goat is armed even on his head. He must be very dangerous if his will is crossed. We must pay him every respect."

Suspicion, however, worked in the mind of the lion cub. He said, "Father, I believe that the goat's overbearing manner is nothing but bluff. Invite him to take a meal with us, and place before him a piece of dried meat. Then we shall see how he can bite."

Next day the goat came into the smithy, demanding that his hoe be repaired immediately. The lion agreed in a most servile manner, which pleased the goat immensely.

"Sir Goat," cringed the lion, "perhaps you will honor us by partaking of a meal while I complete your work."

The goat was flattered and agreed. He was shown into a hut where the meat was placed before him, with the lion cub to wait on him. He tried to eat the dried meat but could not. "Here, cub," he said, "you eat it, for I am accustomed to eating grass and leaves." Then when the hoe was repaired he departed without even a word of thanks or farewell.

That night the lion cub told his father and mother, "There is no need to fear the goat. His teeth are so feeble that he cannot bite, his hooves and horns so blunt that he cannot protect himself. Let us put an end to his pretensions."

Soon the goat was back at the lion's smithy with an axe to be sharpened. "Do this without delay," he shouted.

"I am busy now," replied the lion politely, "but shall be glad to sharpen your axe this afternoon."

"What!" shrieked the goat in a rage. "Do you dare to make me wait? Do you know who I am? I am Sir Goat, the mighty one, terror of animals and men."

Very quietly the lion replied, "Well, Sir Goat, had you been humble and courteous like the other animals of the forest and villages, you would have departed with your work nicely done. Since, however, you assume a position to which you are not entitled, and for which you are not fitted, I shall have to show you who is the mighty one, terror of animals and men." With this he struck the goat to the ground, and that night the lion enjoyed goat meat with his wife and cub.

LOOK BEHIND
AS WELL AS BEFORE

The big white ant, the luswa, wanted to get married and was taking the bride-price to the parents of the girl to whom he was addressing his attentions. He was so occupied with his errand that he did not look behind, or he would have seen a frog following him. The frog was licking his lips as he went after the luswa, and was so intent on the prospect of a feast that he did not see a snake following him. Had the snake looked behind, he would have known that a wooden club was after him. The club was so eager to overtake the snake that he did not see the small white ants doggedly pursuing him. The small white ants, the tuswalandala, did not realize it, but a fowl was on their tracks. The fowl was anxious to feast off the small white ants, but did not know that a wild cat was slinking after her. The wild cat had his eye on the fowl, otherwise he would have detected a trap that was in his path. The trap was thinking of nothing but the wild cat or he would have seen the bush fire rolling toward him. The bush fire was heaving up sparks and smoke and thus failed to realize that water was barring his way. The water only thought of attacking the fire, and so was not prepared for the drought that was on his heels.

The parents of the prospective bride had cooked a feast, but before they could sit down to it the frog began to eat the big white ant. The snake attacked the frog. The club struck down the snake. The small white ants gnawed into the club, the fowl snapped up the small white ants, the wild cat seized the fowl, the trap fell on the wild cat, the fire consumed the trap, the water put out the fire, the drought dried up the water, and all that was left was a dusty waste. How much better if the white ant had looked behind. And moreover, if you have cruel designs upon another, don't forget that others may have similar designs on you.